JUST A LITTLE TASTE

A Moments in Maplesville Novella

Farrah Rochon

Nicobar Press

Cover by Mae Phillips of
CoverFreshDesigns.com
Edited by Karen Dale Harris

ISBN: 978-1-938125-15-7

Special thanks to my brother,
Chef Donnie Roybiskie, Jr.,
for helping me sort through all the food truck details. This story would not have happened without your input.

JUST A LITTLE TASTE

A Moments in Maplesville Novella

Chapter One

Kiera Coleman was stalling.

With good reason.

She had been dreading the meeting to discuss outfitting her food truck since the moment she received an email from her former culinary school partner recommending the person who had renovated his rig. She'd stared in shock at her computer screen for a solid five minutes, sure the name must be a sick, twisted joke.

But it wasn't a twisted joke, just a horrible coincidence.

Trey Watson.

After more than a decade, he was back in Louisiana, back in their small hometown of Maplesville. In less than an hour, she would be face to face with he whom she'd vowed years ago never to think of again.

Instead of pacing back and forth or kicking the wall, she concentrated on her work, praying that it would have the usual calming effect. So far, so good.

As she lifted the lid of the 32-quart aluminum stockpot, she was inundated with a heady blend of garlic, cayenne, and cumin. She inhaled a deep whiff of the spicy aroma, focusing on its essence as it hit the back of her throat. She stirred the tender chunks of chicken breast and Cajun sausage swirling throughout the dark brown stock.

Satisfied that the balance of seasoning in the jambalaya her long-time client, the Chamber of Commerce, had ordered for their monthly meeting was up to par, she scooped in six cups of long-grain rice, gave the mixture another few stirs and slid the lid back in place. Then she marched to the industrial walk-in cooler, one of two in her catering company's main kitchen, and grabbed a stainless steel bowl filled with her special recipe of lump king crab meat, cream cheese and herbs.

As she positioned a fourteen-inch pastry bag inside a funnel, Kiera caught herself whistling Erykah Badu's "Love of My Life." The pastry bag slipped through her fingers, sending the funnel skittering across her prep workstation.

"Dammit," she whispered.

She hadn't so much as thought about that song in years. The nerve of her subconscious to bring it up today of all days.

She righted the pastry bag and, with more force than necessary, began stuffing the crab mixture inside.

"Macy, is the first set of pastry shells ready?" she called out to the only full-time employee she could afford to keep on Catering by Kiera's payroll.

"They're lined up," Macy Bardell answered from right behind her, making Kiera jump. "The next set has about three more minutes in the oven, then I'll slip them into the cooler for a few minutes. Are you ok?"

"Perfect," Kiera said through gritted teeth. "In this heat it's important that the crab tarts are nice and chilled before we transport them. I'll start filling the first set. You get back to the bacon-wrapped dates. Some of them looked on the small side."

"The dates are already done, with more than enough to cover the order." Macy lifted the pastry bag from Kiera's hands. "I'll take care of filling the pastry shells, too. You have more important things to do."

Kiera cast her assistant an annoyed look, which, of course, Macy ignored.

With bright turquoise hair, and tattooed within an inch of her life, Macy was Kiera's complete opposite. Never mind the difference in race—that was a non-factor. Where Kiera was tall and willowy, Macy was short and curvy, and the most outrageous thing Kiera had ever done to her ordinary dark brown hair was adding gold highlights on the same day she had her usual sleek bob trimmed just above her chin. That move had started the tongues around Maplesville wagging.

Their physical contrast was nothing

compared to the difference in their personalities. Macy had enough attitude to choke a lion, while Kiera was normally the queen of playing it cool.

Except for today.

"I don't get why you're not dying to get to your meeting." Macy's left brow lifted, causing the turquoise barbell she had pierced through it to twitch. "You've been looking for someone to remodel the Kiera's Kickin' Kajun food truck for months and this guy came all the way from Houston just to meet with you."

"I can't leave until Sammy delivers the seafood order. I need to work on my recipe for the cook-off later."

"I'll be here to accept the delivery from Sammy. And I already told you that your take on Shrimp Napoleon—turning it into a wrap—is a shoo-in as a finalist. Kiera's Kickin' Kajun is what you need to work on now. If you don't hire someone, you're never going to get it up and running in time."

"I know." Kiera sighed. Deep and dramatic. It had been a long couple of months. She deserved that sigh.

The goal was to have her new food truck operating by the start of the Louisiana Shrimp Festival—less than five weeks away. The three-day event, which took place during the first weekend of September, was slated to have over a hundred thousand hungry visitors. And, if the gods were really smiling down on her, she also would be chosen to compete in the shrimp cook-off. As a finalist Kiera's Kickin' Kajun would be promoted throughout the event. She would have those thousands of festival-goers eating out of the palm of her hand—literally. And, hopefully, she would top off the weekend by winning the $25,000 top prize.

Yeah, that was a lot of dreaming, but dreaming was the first step, wasn't it?

"I say get to your meeting and snap this guy up before someone else does," Macy said as she filled a second pastry bag. "From what you've told me he's a genius at renovations."

Kiera snorted. "I doubt I used the word genius."

"You raved about the job he did on your friend's food truck, *and* he's local. This guy sounds perfect."

This guy.

If she wrote up a list of guys she never wanted to encounter ever again, *this guy* would hold spots one through ten.

She couldn't dispute Trey Watson's talent. He'd performed magic on her friend Mychal Dickerson's food truck. When she scrolled through the before and after pictures her culinary school partner had forwarded her, she'd been blown away.

And, yes, Trey was local. At least temporarily. It was that particular tidbit that sent a lightening bolt of unease racing down Kiera's spine. Of all the custom renovators in all the world, why did *he* have to be her only hope of having her food truck ready in time?

She'd spent the past several months researching outfits across the country that specialized in mobile kitchen renovations, but either they were too far away, too expensive, or they wanted to sell her an already-outfitted truck.

She couldn't afford to buy a brand new food truck. She needed someone local who would renovate the truck she'd already purchased for a ridiculously high price. Sight unseen. From a guy on Craigslist.

She needed Trey Watson. The sooner, the better.

Lord, help her.

She glanced over to find Macy staring at her with another of those challenging looks. Kiera held her hands up in surrender. "Alright, alright. I'm going. But don't get your hopes up. He might be too expensive."

"Think positive. The sooner you show him what he's working with, the sooner we can have Kiera's Kickin' Kajun out on the street making money. Now, go."

Kiera trudged to her office at the rear of the corrugated building that housed the company she'd started five years ago. Owning her own catering business had always been her dream, but she didn't feel like a success yet. Probably because she hadn't worked as hard as some people probably thought she should have, even though she'd balanced her catering with a full-time job as a public affairs research analyst up until a few months ago.

She'd gotten much of the seed money to start the business from her share of her late father's life insurance, and what that didn't cover, her older brother, Mason, had. Just a few months ago, Mason had once again come to her rescue, loaning her enough money for renovations and the kitchen equipment needed for the food truck, after she'd sunk all of her savings into buying the actual truck. From Craigslist. For $20,000.

Cash.

"What were you thinking?" Kiera whispered, closing her office door and lightly thumping the back of her head against it.

That was the problem; she hadn't been thinking. She had been so damn eager to get a piece of New Orleans's growing food truck market that she didn't give a second thought to purchasing a truck she only saw in pictures posted online. Sure, she noticed a few dents and scrapes, but she figured with just a little elbow grease, Kiera's Kickin' Kajun would be hitting the highway in no time flat.

Yeah, well, that hadn't worked out quite the way she planned.

Estimates for getting the truck up to code

ranged anywhere from another thirty to another fifty thousand dollars. She tried to take out a loan, but Mason convinced her it made more financial sense to borrow the money from him, interest free.

Kiera couldn't argue with his logic, but she was so damn tired of being indebted to him. She was thirty-two years old. When would she stop looking to her big brother to bail her out?

"Right now," she said in a fierce whisper.

She had a plan this time—a well-thought-out plan. The contract she'd just signed with the Magnolia Ridge Country Club to cater several of the huge galas they held throughout the year would be a significant boost to her company's profits. And if things went the way she envisioned with the food truck, she would be able to pay Mason back in less than a year, *with* interest. Though Kiera knew her brother would swim through a river of honey and let an army of fire ants snack on him before he accepted interest from his baby sister.

The ability to repay Mason was important, but it wasn't the most crucial part of her plan. What *really* mattered was that, if she played her cards right, she would soon be solidly on the road to realizing her ultimate dream, owning her own restaurant.

The first step was getting Kiera's Kickin' Kajun up and running. Ever since Mychal had regaled her with tales of the mind-blowing business he was doing with his food truck in Austin, Texas, Kiera had been clamoring to tap into that market. New Orleans's food truck community wasn't nearly as robust as Austin's, but in the last year it had grown exponentially. She wanted to be at the forefront, and every day her truck sat idle it was another day she fell behind.

She'd finally secured everything she needed—the truck, the NSA-certified kitchen equipment, even the company that would shrink-wrap the logo around the truck's exterior. All she needed was someone to put it all together.

Trey Watson.

She managed to contain her sigh this time, but just barely.

It had been fourteen years since she'd last spoken to him, so she hadn't known what to expect when she'd sent the initial email asking if he was available to work on her renovation. She'd rewritten it at least a half-dozen times, changing the tone from lighthearted and friendly to severely professional. In the end, she'd settled on informal and efficient.

She'd prepared herself for a range of responses. Anger. Resentment. Indifference.

Instead, his response had been simply…Trey.

There was no other way to describe it. Even in those few words, letting her know that he'd just finished a job and could be in Maplesville in a matter of days to check out her truck, Kiera had gotten a sense of the carefree, laid back boy who had captured her heart. And then broke it.

She pressed a hand to her stomach, trying to quell the queasy dread she felt every time she thought about putting her dreams in his hands. Again.

Dammit. It shouldn't matter that it was Trey. Their brief time together, while the most intense romance she had ever experienced, had ended back when she was still a starry-eyed girl.

She was a professional now, and this was business. *Her* business.

Getting the Kiera's Kickin' Kajun food truck up and running before the shrimp festival was paramount to her plans. If it meant temporarily working with the man who represented both the best and worst of her past, that's just something she would have to do.

Lord, help her.

Kiera pulled into the entrance of the industrial park where she'd told Trey to meet her. She immediately spotted a black quad-cab pick-up with massive chrome wheels and a gleaming silver stripe that rimmed the exterior. A warm, almond brown arm, roped with tight muscles and glistening with sweat, hung out the driver's side window. A colorful serpent tattoo she hadn't seen in years wound its way down to the wrist.

She caught sight of his tapered fingers drumming a rhythm on the door panel. Suddenly all she could think of was the myriad ways those skillful fingers used to drive her wild.

Kiera groaned.

This was going to be torture. Pure, sweet torture.

Get it together.

She honked her horn twice, and motioned for Trey to follow. The owner of the industrial park was a good friend of Mason's and he allowed her to keep her truck parked on the undeveloped lot at the rear of the property.

She pulled up next to the twenty-six-foot former moving truck she'd purchased several months ago. Kiera struggled to stave off the wave of disappointment that tended to wash over her whenever she laid eyes on the truck.

It was the high hopes she'd had for this venture, juxtaposed against it's current reality—a dilapidated truck with rust spots as big as her head—that made this situation so hard to stomach. The truck would have to be completely overhauled if it had any chance of ever getting on the road.

But she refused to wallow in her foolish mistake any longer. It was done. Thanks to her brother—yet again—she now had the capital to move forward with her plans.

Kiera glanced in her rearview mirror and saw the door to Trey's truck open. He stepped out and her stomach flip-flopped.

"Good Lord," she breathed.

He still looked like her Trey. Except fourteen years had made him fourteen times sexier.

How was that even possible?

Her finger hovered over her Mazda CX-5's push-button start mechanism as she continued to watch Trey through her rearview mirror. His lean frame strolling toward her with that easy, confident stride that she remembered so well momentarily mesmerized her.

He stopped a couple of feet from her door, and Kiera had to talk herself out of throwing the car in reverse and saying *to hell* with this meeting.

Stop it! She was not the same foolish, love-struck girl Trey Watson walked away from all those years ago. She could do this.

She shut off the engine, got out of her car, and turned to Trey.

And had the breath knocked out of her.

Oh, God, yes. He was still her Trey.

Tall and lean, but solid and sinewy, with buttery smooth skin that stretched tight over well-defined muscles. If she closed her eyes and concentrated hard enough, she could still taste his spicy, unique flavor on her tongue.

He took off his sunglasses and smiled the panty-dropping smile that used to convince her to do things she couldn't think about now without blushing.

"How're you doing, Slim?"

Things inside her went liquid as the nickname he'd given her all those years ago rolled off his tongue. Thinking of his tongue immediately conjured images she'd spent the better part of a decade trying to banish.

"I'm fine," Kiera managed to say, her voice cracking slightly. She swallowed and tried again. "How about you?"

He shrugged a well-sculpted shoulder. "You know me. I'm always good."

Yes. He was. Every single time she'd been with him, he had always been more than just good. He'd been the very best.

He'd also been the very worst.

Of all the people Mychal could have recommended, why, why, *why* did it have to be Trey?

Not that she was all that surprised that Trey was in the business of fixing cars. The summer they were together, he spent countless hours restoring that stupid Pontiac GTO he bought with the money he earned at Decker Anderson's auto body shop in neighboring Gauthier. She remembered the first time he took the GTO out for a spin and got suckered into a drag race and cracked the car up against a tree.

He was so damn reckless. With everything. Her heart included.

Trey Watson was the epitome of a bad boy, which is why she had been so drawn to him from the very beginning. He was the boy that every girl had been warned against. The one who could make a girl's knees go weak with just his smile, and make those same knees spread open with just a few sweetly whispered words.

She should know.

Stop thinking about that!

Kiera shook her head to get her mind off things she had no business thinking about right now.

"Thanks for meeting with me." She gestured toward the truck. "Let me show you around."

"Whoa. That's all I get after all these years?"

"This is business, Trey. I have a very tight schedule and there's a lot of work to be done."

His jaw went rigid and the smile that had glinted in his eyes just a second ago faded.

Kiera gave him a wide berth as she headed for the back of the truck. Before she could unlock the padlock hanging from the back door, Trey plucked the keys from her fingers and did it for her.

"What are you doing with a food truck anyway?" he asked as he drew the lock shackle from the fastener. "I thought you went to school in psychology or some shit like that?"

Some shit like that…

It was such a Trey thing to say.

"I was a political science major. I went to culinary school after I got my degree. I own my own catering company now. I want to branch out by adding a food truck component to it."

He peered at her over his shoulder. "I'm glad to hear all those recipes you used to test out on me weren't because you wanted to give me heartburn for being such a dick." She opened her mouth to protest, but Trey stopped her. "That was a joke. I used to enjoy your cooking. Except for that one time," he tacked on.

Kiera felt her cheeks heat. She knew exactly what he was talking about. The time he'd gotten food poisoning when she'd ambitiously tried to replicate Julia Child's bouillabaisse recipe.

"I apologized for that," Kiera said. "Besides, you didn't have to eat it."

A hint of that sexy smile reappeared. "You know I always had a hard time saying no to you."

Except for the one time he did.

The stark reminder of what he'd done to her heart was exactly what she needed to remind her to keep this strictly about business.

She pointed to the truck. "I have to get back to my kitchen soon. If you don't mind, I'd like to get on with this."

His whiskey-colored eyes examined her for several long, heart-stopping seconds before he braced his hand on the inside of the door and propelled himself up and inside the truck. He held a hand out for her.

Kiera faltered for the briefest moment. Of course, he caught her hesitation. And, being Trey, *of course* he wouldn't let her get away with that without remarking on it.

"Don't be afraid. You know I don't bite unless you ask me to."

Her body shuddered in response to his silkily spoken words. When she looked up, she caught the cocky smile tilting his lips.

This was such *a bad idea.*

With an inward sigh, Kiera accepted his hand and he hauled her into the truck.

"Alright," he said. "Show me what I'm working with."

He stood with his feet braced apart and those muscled arms crossed over his chest. The early August heat turned the inside of the truck into a sauna, and the thick humidity caused a fine sheen of sweat to glisten on his warm brown skin.

No question about it; this was a *very* bad idea.

Trying her best to suppress these feelings she did not want to be feeling right now—or ever—Kiera guided Trey around the twenty-five-by-eight-foot space, explaining the layout she'd envisioned in her head.

"I want the hot prep area and the cold prep area to be on opposite sides." She waved her hands around the middle portion of the truck's left wall. "The three-compartment sink will go here. I already have that, the cold condiment station and the steaming table stored in Mason's garage. The only big purchase I haven't made yet is the warming oven."

"You putting in a fryer?"

"I have a two basket one on order. It should be delivered by the end of the week." She walked toward the center of the truck. "Now, I know most people have the cooler toward the front, but I want my veggies for the wraps to be as crisp as possible, so it makes more sense for me to put the refrigeration closer to the prep area." She turned to him. "The menu will mostly consist of Cajun favorites done in a wrap form. I have a jambalaya wrap, shrimp creole wrap, so on and so forth."

Kiera felt as if she was rambling, but being in such close proximity to Trey had turned her normally cool and collected disposition on its head.

"Interesting spin," was all he said.

"My catering company specializes in Cajun cuisine. I wanted to continue with the theme, but do something that was more portable and easier to eat on the go."

And she was rambling again.

Why did she feel as if she needed to justify her menu choices to him? He was here to renovate her truck; what he thought about her menu had no bearing on any of this. Though, it wasn't as if he had asked her to justify anything. She was the one who suddenly couldn't shut up.

"You should consider a beverage cooler," Trey said. "If you get one of the smaller ones it won't take up much space and it'll stay cool enough to keep your vegetables crisp."

"Are you sure that would work?"

"I can make it work," he said. A roguish grin curved up one corner of his mouth. "I'm good at what I do, Slim. I shouldn't have to tell you that."

Kiera's eyes fell shut as tremors of awareness skirted along her skin.

"Don't do this, Trey." She opened her eyes and fixed him with her sternest glare. "I already told you, this is business. Strictly business. Don't think you're going to come in here with those pretty brown eyes and that sexy little smile and make me fall for you again. There will be no strolls down memory lane, you got that?"

His left brow arched. "If I recall correctly, *you're* the one who pursued *me* back then."

He was right; she had.

Young, stupid, and trying her best to rebel against Mason's overbearing protectiveness, she'd set out to land the one boy she knew Mason would object to the most. She'd had no idea what she had been getting herself into back then.

But that was in the past. She wasn't that girl

anymore. Whether or not Trey Watson was still that same wild, reckless boy didn't matter. That's not what she wanted from him.

"Look, getting this food truck off the ground is important to my business. If you're not going to take this seriously, I'll find someone else to work on the truck."

Though, she had no idea who. She didn't have time to find anyone else. Trey was her last hope.

Despite that, Kiera turned and headed for the back door.

Trey's hand on her shoulder stopped her. Heat radiated from the spot he touched, singeing her nerve endings and setting off a low burn within her belly.

In a voice tinged with contrition, Trey said, "Okay, fine. Strictly business."

Kiera looked back at him, her eyes narrowing with skepticism.

He put both hands up. "I promise. No funny business. I'm all about work."

"Good," she said with a nod.

The edge of his mouth lifted the tiniest bit, sending yet another round of flutters to quake through her belly. With a sexy wink, he said, "I think I'm going to like you being the boss."

Chapter Two

Trey observed Kiera as she walked around the exterior of the truck, pointing out where the features of the custom-designed shrink-wrap would be displayed. He tried like hell to keep his outward expression neutral, but the emotions tumbling inside of him had his stomach in knots.

When he read her email requesting a meeting to discuss a truck renovation, Trey thought it was the perfect opportunity to show her the kind of success the boy who wasn't good enough for her had made of himself. He'd even turned down a job on another truck in order to come back to Maplesville and meet with her.

But that spurt of vindictiveness had quickly started to wither away. It crumbled completely the moment she stepped out of her car. Despite everything that went down with them all those years ago, the thought of being cruel to Kiera in any way made his stomach hurt.

"You have to make sure the window cutout is precise," Kiera said. "And right here is where I want a chalkboard built into the side so I can write the day's menu and specials."

"Whatever you say, Boss."

She shot another of those exasperated looks

his way, wringing a low chuckle from him. He'd lost count of how many times he'd been on the receiving end of that look in the past half-hour. He'd told her that if their dealings were to be strictly about business, then he would address her accordingly.

Apparently, she didn't appreciate his humor.

Trey was laughing now, but earlier, when he'd gotten his first good look at her after fourteen years, laughing had been the furthest thing from his mind.

In a life full of regrets, letting Kiera Coleman go had always been his biggest.

It took him a long time to admit it, but he had never gotten over her. Not even close. He never imagined that he would find his soul mate so early in life, but he'd found that with Kiera.

He still remembered the afternoon she'd first approached him, her two girlfriends, Callie Webber and Jada Dangerfield, looking on in alarmed fascination. Trey had suspected something was up from the moment the normally timid Kiera had sidled up to him and asked if he wanted to take her out for a hamburger after the Friday night football game. Back then, there was only one reason a little goody-two-shoes hottie like Kiera Coleman would want anything to do with a guy like him: she wanted to take a walk on the wild side.

He'd been wrong. She'd told him point

blank that her reason for asking him out was to piss off her older brother, who had embarrassed her the week before by threatening to beat up her date for the senior homecoming dance. Trey was payback, nothing more.

He had been willing to give her what she wanted. Despite the fact that she had been three years younger and ninety-eight pounds of surefire jailbait, Trey had jumped at the chance to start something up with Kiera.

Never in his wildest dreams had he expected to fall so damn hard for her.

It had come as a shock to both he and Kiera. But the connection had been there from their very first date, when they'd sat in the parking lot of the high school football stadium, holed up in his dad's old pickup that he'd been forced to drive back then. They'd talked until the maintenance workers had arrived the next morning to repair the damage the teams had done to the field the previous night.

For the six months that followed, he and Kiera had been Maplesville's most unlikely couple: a boy from the wrong side of the tracks and a girl who had everything going for her. Despite the odds being stacked against them, there had been no doubt in Trey's mind that Kiera would be the woman he spent the rest of his life with.

But shit happened. Especially in his life.

The last decade had been just a bunch of shit

happening, one incident after the other. He'd come full circle, returning to his hometown of Maplesville after all these years. It gave him the opportunity to make a fresh start and maybe get things right this time.

Getting a call from the girl who'd gotten away was a boon—one he probably didn't deserve—but he was taking it.

Not that he thought Kiera would simply fall into his arms, and honestly, he wasn't sure if he even wanted that. His and Kiera's relationship had started out as a farce. Based on how it ended, Trey wasn't sure if it had ever turned into something real for her.

Still, it couldn't change the way he felt about her, even after all this time.

As Kiera made her way around the truck, Trey studied the woman she had become. She wore her hair much shorter these days, in a sexy cut that had the ends brushing against her high cheekbones. Streaks of honey gold contrasted with her dark brown hair. The highlights made her caramel-colored skin glow.

Trey couldn't help but appreciate the way her dark jeans stretched across those thighs he used to dream about at night. He'd always been a leg man. He loved long, willowy ones that could wrap around his waist. Kiera had legs like that. She also had a mouth like an angel. And, as with all great mouths, with just a little coaxing he could get her to do the naughtiest things with it.

Trey swallowed a moan.

"You okay?" Kiera asked.

"Yeah, sure." He gestured to the truck. "You mind if I take a look underneath the hood?"

"If you want to." She shrugged. "My mechanic already checked it out. It was leaking oil, but that's been fixed."

As he tilted the engine hood toward him, Trey ignored the ridiculous flash of jealousy that gripped him at the thought of another mechanic putting his hands on her truck. They had not seen each other in fourteen years. He would be foolish to think another man had not touched *more* than just her truck.

He shook off the disturbing thought and poked at the engine, relieved to see that it was indeed in good shape. He would have enough on his hands trying to get the interior renovated within the short timeframe she'd given him; he didn't need mechanical issues, too.

"I've got a question," Trey asked as he pushed the hood back up over the engine. "Why didn't you just buy an already renovated truck? Probably would have made more sense."

"I thought I could save money buying something that I could fix up."

Trey dusted off his hands. "I hope this didn't set you back much. It's not worth more than a couple of thousand."

Her silence caused his curiosity to perk up.

"How much did you pay for this truck, Kiera?"

"That's not important."

"Tell me anyway."

She blew out an irritated breath. "Twenty-thousand."

Trey felt his jaw go slack before he burst out laughing. "Twenty-thousand dollars for *this*? Babe, you got screwed nice and hard in that deal, and not in a good way."

Kiera held both hands up. "You know what? Forget it. I'll get somebody else to work on the truck."

He caught her by the wrist and turned her around to face him. "Would you stop doing that?"

"I'm not going to stand here and let you make fun of me, Trey."

"I'm not making fun of you."

"Yes, you are. You get off on making fun of me. Always have."

"Wrong. I got off on doing something else entirely to you, darling."

Trey knew he'd crossed a line the moment the words came out of his mouth. Lingering resentment over the way things ended between them was causing him to be unnecessarily obnoxious, and he needed to put a lid on it.

Kiera jerked her wrist away from him, her eyes shooting daggers. She stepped up to him and pointed a slender finger at his chest.

"Let's get something clear right now. If we're going to work together on this, then you're going to stop twisting everything I say into some kind of sexual play on words. You got that?"

Her breaths came out shallow and rapid, the same way they used to after one of their epic arguments—arguments that usually ended with the two of them tearing each other's clothes off and going at it like a couple of horny kids. Which, of course, is what they were back then. Trey had a feeling that wasn't happening today.

"I got it," he answered, but he didn't back away.

"I mean it, Trey. I need to know whether or not you can handle a professional working relationship, because I don't have to put up with this."

She was right. If this were anyone else seeking to hire him, he would never have made that remark.

"You're right," Trey said. "That was completely out of line. Just because we used to…well, you know…it doesn't give me the right to talk to you that way. It won't happen again."

She studied him for several moments, her expression still holding a hint of distrust. Trey couldn't blame her. Keeping that promise would be hard as hell.

Kiera returned their discussion to the truck's interior. When she mentioned her concern about a lack of counter space between the steam table and drain board, Trey said, "I've got a fix that can double your prep area. It's a fold-down countertop. It should work here."

There was a skeptical hitch to her brow when she asked, "Do you have pictures?"

"I can do you one better. Come home with me and I'll show you first-hand." Kiera's mouth opened, but Trey quickly stopped her before she could protest. "That's not what I meant." *Shit.* "My home *is* my work."

Trey sensed her reluctance, but after a few moments she nodded and got into her car.

They headed west and soon crossed the railroad tracks that cut off the northwestern edge of Maplesville from the rest of town. It was the one area that had remained relatively unchanged. There was nothing but sugarcane farms and a junkyard out this way; he wasn't surprised that businesses weren't eager to build here.

They turned onto the dirt and gravel road that led to his family's property. Trey drove past the white clapboard house where he and his older sister, Lori, grew up with their asshole of a father. That is, until years of inhaling dust while working at the local cement plant—something he'd harped on Trey to do instead of 'wasting his time' working on cars—and a three-pack-a-day habit caught up with him back in Trey's senior year of high school. It was only fair that the lung cancer that had killed his mother five years before would come back to take his old man's life.

Lori had moved to St. Louis as soon as Trey graduated from high school. Neither of them had bothered to try selling the old house; it wasn't as if potential buyers were lighting up the phone line putting in offers to buy.

Trey continued to the back of the property, pulling his truck up next to the 1963 Bluebird School Bus he'd purchased from a junkyard for five-hundred dollars a couple of years ago. He climbed out of his pick-up and leaned against the rear bumper, waiting for Kiera. She drove up next to him, and rolled down her window.

"What is this?" she asked.

"You said you wanted to see more of my work."

"This is a school bus."

"Come inside." That suspicious look returned to her eyes. "I won't try anything, Kiera."

She climbed out from behind the wheel of her compact SUV, watching him as if he was a cobra ready to strike. She remained two steps behind as he walked over to the bus and opened the door.

Trey swung his hand out in a sweeping gesture. "After you."

Her stare still filled with distrust, she climbed the steps of the bus, turned, and gasped.

"Oh, my God!" Her eyes flew to his. "You

did this?"

He nodded. "If you want to see exactly what I can do when it comes to renovations, this is the best example." He climbed up the steps and motioned for her to move further into the space. "Go ahead," he encouraged. "Check it out."

Trey couldn't stem the pride pumping through his veins as Kiera surveyed his home, her eyes filled with awe. She ran her fingers along the gleaming Australian cypress that covered the floors, walls and ceiling.

"This is amazing," she murmured.

The first half of the bus was an open kitchen, living room, and dining room area. He'd made the most of the limited space, modifying the appliances as best he could so they would fit and building shelving that ran along the entire rim of the bus's interior. The living room furniture was upholstered in dark brown leather, adding to the opulent feel.

"This is what I wanted to show you," Trey said, walking over to the custom countertops that folded down to create more counter space. "I can do something like this in your food truck."

"That would be perfect," Kiera said. She flipped the countertop back and forth a few times. "How long have you lived here?"

"A couple of years. It started as a hobby. I went to an auto show a few years back and someone had tricked out one of those old conversion vans, like the one Mr. Pratt used to drive to school."

"Ah, the Scooby Doo Mystery Van. I remember it well."

"Yep. Just like that one. I decided I would try to do the same thing, but on a larger scale. I bought this bus and spent about a year working on it. I never thought I'd be living in it, but things worked out that way."

She looked over at him, her raised brows inviting him to elaborate.

"I was a partner in an engine repair business with a good friend back in Houston, but I was forced to sell my share in the business."

Yet another instance of the shit that had become a normal part of his existence.

Trey shrugged. "I'd gotten tired of working on engines anyway. And I discovered that I'm pretty good at this conversion thing."

"I think you're amazing at it, but I thought you renovated mainly food trucks?"

"So far it's been mostly food trucks; they're what's in demand right now. There aren't many people lining up to live in a converted bus, and honestly, for the amount of money I put into it, I could have bought something much bigger, but this is the best example I have of the kind of work I can do. It also makes for a pretty cool house that I can drive wherever my work takes me."

"It's a very cool house," she said. "You have

an amazing talent."

If she paid him one more compliment Trey was sure his chest would burst. He'd probably given tours of his home to over a hundred people—friends, people in the mobile home conversion business—and they all had reacted with the same kind of awe. There was just something about getting that kind of praise from Kiera—*his* Kiera—that made it so much more special.

"It suits you," she said. "You never struck me as the 'house with a picket fence and two-point-five kids' kind of guy."

Trey swallowed the response that nearly escaped his lips. Instead, he asked, "So, what do you think? You willing to trust me with your food truck?"

She blew out a heavy breath before she turned to him and crossed her arms over her chest. "It will all depend on the cost. After seeing this, I'm not sure I can afford you."

"I'm sure that brother of yours will be willing to front you some cash."

Her smooth skin tightened over her cheekbones as the friendly mood that had occupied this space just a second ago evaporated.

"Mason doesn't have anything to do with this," she said. "Let me know your price and I'll let you know whether or not the renovation is a go."

"My price is negotiable. Why don't you tell me what you can afford?"

"Let me worry about what I can afford. Tell me your price and we can negotiate from there."

Well, one thing hadn't changed; she was still stubborn as hell.

"Give me until tomorrow to work up an estimate. I'll crunch some numbers based on the things you pointed out today. You think you can email me a list of the equipment you already have?"

She nodded, and her eyes softened just a touch. "I haven't really thanked you for agreeing to do this, but know that I appreciate it. When I made the decision to contact you, I knew this would be...well, awkward. How could it not be after all this time?" She put a hand on his forearm. "But I'm happy I called. I need this food truck to succeed, and after seeing the kind of work you can do, I know I made the right decision."

Trey's skin heated where she touched him. That's all it took, one simple touch.

His lungs constricted as their gazes locked. The full weight of this moment, of once again occupying the same space with her, breathing the same air she breathed, hit him square in the chest.

He lifted the hair off her right cheek and tucked it behind her ear. "Damn, it's good to see you again, Slim."

Her eyes dropped to his lips and lingered there for several heartbeats. The air in the Bluebird seemed to evaporate, leaving nothing but intense awareness pulsing around them.

"It's good to see you, too," she said, her voice hoarse. Sexy.

Time stood still, then it crawled backwards, to years ago when the woman standing before him was a young, innocent, stunningly beautiful girl. A girl who'd wrapped herself around his heart and hadn't let go, even after all these years.

Regret, deep and wide and soul breaking, gripped his chest, clutching so tight Trey could barely breathe. He'd lived with regret over the way things had ended with Kiera for so long, he thought he'd gotten used to it. But being here with her brought back all the remorse he'd suffered for taking the easy way out and not fighting for their love.

Was this his chance to make up for the way he'd left?

"Do you want to hang out for a while?" Trey asked. "Maybe we can have a beer, talk a bit?" He took a step closer. "Come on, Slim," he said, brushing the backs of his fingers along her smooth jawline. "It's been a long time. We've got a lot to catch up on."

Her chest heaved with the pronounced breath she sucked in. She took two steps back and wrapped her arms around her waist.

"No," she said, shaking her head. "No. I…I

have to go."

Disappointment pummeled his chest.

"Kiera—"

"I'll get that email out to you as soon as I can," she said as she backed away from him like a frightened kitten. "Let me know when you have the estimate ready. And remember my timetable. The shrimp festival is less than five weeks away."

With that she turned and left him standing in the middle of his living room. Apparently, when it came to strolling down memory lane, Kiera wasn't particularly interested. But after seeing her again, Trey was all too ready to take that journey.

Kiera carried the chocolate torte she'd bought from Jada's favorite bakery up the porch steps of Callie's brown and white creole cottage in one of Maplesville's older neighborhoods. This area had managed to avoid the rapid growth most of the town had undergone in the last few years.

Callie opened the door before she could knock and planted a kiss on Kiera's cheek. "Seems as if I haven't seen you in forever," her friend said.

"Not since last month at Jada's," Kiera returned. "Any sign of her yet?"

Callie nodded toward the driveway. "Pulling up as we speak."

They both stood in the doorway watching as the third member of their trio parked behind Kiera's SUV.

Kiera and her two best friends, Jada Dangerfield and Callie Webber, were meeting at Callie's for their monthly wine, dessert and gossip session—a tradition that started several years ago, after Callie's husband left her for a younger woman.

"Hello, my lovelies," Jada called, shouldering her bag as she kicked her car door closed. She hurried over to them and issued out kisses. "How are you two doing?"

"I think the question of the day is how are *you* doing?" Kiera said. "You have some news to announce, don't you?"

With a squeal, Jada stuck out her left hand and showcased the two-and-a-half carat cushion cut diamond engagement ring Kiera had helped Mason pick out last week.

"Oh, my God!" Callie gasped. "I didn't realize he was going to ask so soon."

"He popped the question at the beach house in Biloxi Saturday night," Jada said. "Great going on the ring, Kiera. It's perfect."

"Well, you did send me at least a dozen pictures."

"Yeah, but I didn't know which one he would pick."

"I think Mason did a great job." Callie twisted Jada's left hand from side to side so she could look at the ring from various angles. "This is gorgeous." She enveloped Jada in a hug. "Congratulations, honey. I'm so happy for the two of you."

"So am I," Kiera said, joining in the hug. "Who would have ever imagined you and Mason would end up together?"

"No one," all three of them said simultaneously, and burst out laughing.

They went into the house and dug into the decadent torte while Jada gave them a play-by-play of Mason's proposal, which included a moonlit picnic on the beach. Kiera was rather stunned to hear the lengths her normally serious brother had gone to in order to make Jada's proposal special.

The discussion naturally segued into a discussion of Callie's upcoming wedding to her fiancé Stefan, which they had decided would take place on an island in Turks and Caicos over the Thanksgiving holiday.

Kiera was happy for her friends. Honestly, she was. They'd both been through horrible divorces with husbands who'd treated them like dirt. But, dammit, at least they'd already had a chance at married life. Of the three of them, *she* was the one who'd always believed in a happily ever after. Even after suffering the trauma of heartbreak at Trey's hand, she'd never lost sight of love. Yet, she was the one who had yet to experience a man dropping to one knee and pledging his love and life to her.

Fortunately, she stopped obsessing over her happily ever after a long time ago. She might not have given up completely, but it wasn't a priority anymore.

Her last serious boyfriend, Garrett Benson, had turned out to be a possessive, clingy jerk whose main goal in life was seeing how far he could climb the social ladder. As if Maplesville's social ladder was all that high to climb.

She no longer had the patience or energy to expend on waiting for Prince Charming to come and whisk her away. She had other things to concentrate on, like growing her business.

"Where'd you get this wine?" Jada asked, peering at the goblet of zinfandel she held up toward the light in Callie's living room.

"I stumbled upon this adorable wine bar when I met Stefan for lunch in New Orleans the other day." A light entered Callie's eyes just at the mention of her fiancé. "They have an awesome selection. We'll need to take one of our Girl's Night In on the road one of these days and hang out there."

"I'm working downtown at the Fortier Foundation three days a week," Jada said. "Maybe we can meet one day after work."

"Sounds like a plan," Kiera said, holding her glass up so they could toast to it.

She and Callie had been friends since elementary school. Jada had moved to Maplesville during their sophomore year of high school. Petite, gorgeous, and a cheerleader to boot, she instantly became one of the most popular girls in school. Callie and Kiera had hated Jada on the spot, until the day they found her defacing the head cheerleader's locker, whom they hated even more.

After that, the three of them had become inseparable. They'd supported each other through numerous heartbreaks, the death of parents and disaster dates.

The disaster dates were now a thing of the past for Callie and Jada, both having found love in the past year. It was particularly astonishing that the person Jada had found love with was Kiera's older brother, Mason. For years the two could hardly stand being in the same room with each other.

Kiera folded her legs underneath her as she settled into the comfy chair she always commandeered at Callie's. She tried to pay attention as Jada filled them in on her new job with a local non-profit, but only listened with half an ear. Much of her mental energy was taken up by what had transpired in her brief visit to Trey's home this afternoon.

Who would have thought the hell raiser who used to hotwire the mayor's car and take it for joyrides would turn into a successful business-owner with a knack for turning decrepit old vehicles into mobile works of art? She thought she'd prepared herself for the emotional overload she knew would come when she first laid eyes on him after fourteen years, but Kiera now realized that nothing could have fully prepared her for the life force that was Trey Watson.

She'd told herself over and over again not to get pulled in by him. He was bad for her in so many ways—mentally, emotionally. She *knew* this! But when faced with his devastating smile and that relentless charm, it was hard to remember exactly *why* he was so bad for her. All she could think about were the multitude of ways he had been so very, very good.

"Kiera!"

She jerked to attention and looked over to find both of her friends staring at her. "What?" she asked.

Jada dropped her head in her hands. "Please don't start this spacing out shit on us again, Kiera."

"I did not space out."

"I called your name three times."

Callie reached over and covered her hand. "You would tell us if something was wrong, wouldn't you?"

The concern in Callie's voice tugged at her heart, but Kiera had decided before she arrived that she wasn't ready to tell her friends about

Trey's return. Jada and Callie had both cautioned her against dating him from the very beginning. Even when things between her and Trey had turned serious, her friends had both been concerned that he would break her heart.

In the ultimate display of true friendship, neither had bothered to say *I told you so* when he eventually did. They'd simply sat by her side, providing an endless supply of tissues and damning Trey Watson to hell.

No, she didn't think telling Jada and Callie about Trey's return to Maplesville was a good idea.

"Would you two please stop looking at me like that," Kiera said. "I'm fine."

"Forgive us if we don't automatically believe you when you say you're fine," Jada said. "You're track record isn't the best."

"Yeah, Kiera," Callie said. "The last time you were acting this way was when you were suckered into that bad deal on Craigslist for the food truck. Is something else going on with the business? Do you need help?"

"No," Kiera said, grimacing at the defensiveness in her voice. "I'm good," she said. "Really. I just landed a catering contract with the Magnolia Ridge Country Club, I'm close to nailing down my recipe for the Louisiana Shrimp Festival, and best of all, Kiera's Kickin' Kajun will soon be operational. Everything in my world is peachy, so stop worrying about me.

I'm a big girl, I can take care of myself."

The expressions on their faces told Kiera neither of her friends had been swayed. Jada's words confirmed it.

"Everything is peachy?" Her future sister-in-law asked with a snort. "Yeah, and I'm the freaking Queen of England."

Kiera blew out a tired breath. They both knew her way too well.

"Look, I just have a lot on my mind, okay." She came up with the one excuse she knew her friends would buy. "I haven't perfected my Shrimp Napoleon wrap recipe yet and I'm starting to freak out a little. The recipe is due to the festival's committee soon."

"*That's* what you're worried about?" Jada asked. "Girl, please."

"I can't help *but* worry," Kiera said. "I really want to win that cook-off so that I can pay Mason back the money he loaned me as soon as possible."

"You know he's not thinking about that money." Jada waved off her concern before draining her wineglass. "Honestly, you'll probably have to tackle him to the ground and literally ram the check down his throat to make him take it."

"If that's my only option, then so be it," Kiera said. "The only reason I accepted the loan to renovate the truck is because he promised he would let me pay him back."

Jada put her hands up. "You can try, but I don't have to tell you how stubborn your brother is."

Kiera fully expected a battle of epic proportion when it came time to pay Mason back. There was no doubt he would find every reason in the world for her to keep the money: She should put it in her nest egg, reinvest it in her business, put it on the side for a rainy day.

A measly twenty thousand dollars was nothing to Mason, who made a phenomenal living as a tax attorney at a high-powered firm in New Orleans. For him, loaning her that money was just another opportunity for him to take care of her.

When their father died of a heart attack when she was eleven-years-old, Mason had taken it upon himself to take care of both her and their mother, despite the fact that he was only fourteen at the time. She knew Mason was only doing what he'd promised their father he would do, but it was time for him to step out of that role. She wasn't a little girl anymore.

Of course, it would be easier for him to stop treating her like a little girl if she didn't need him to bail her out all the damn time.

She was done with that, too.

She'd meant what she'd said earlier today. If she couldn't make this food truck venture happen on her own, then it would not happen at all.

Of course, just the thought of her newest business venture immediately conjured thoughts of the man she'd hired to help her get it off the ground. The image of that glistening tattoo flashed before her mind's eye, and Kiera had to bite back a moan.

God, but she didn't want to deal with the complications Trey brought into her life. Just the sound of his voice caused feelings she'd buried a long time ago to reemerge.

Trey wasn't just bad for her peace of mind; he was dangerous. He'd led her astray more times than she could count, and with just the hint of his sexy smile and a crook of his finger, Kiera feared she would be all too willing to follow him down the delicious path to destruction again.

Chapter Three

Trey had just passed his dad's old tool shed when he caught sight of a cardboard box in his rearview mirror. The Bluebird didn't have an address, so he'd used the house's address. The deliveryman had set it on the back kitchen steps.

He stomped on the break, threw the truck in reverse, and backed up to the house. Once he got to the Bluebird, Trey didn't even bother going inside. He set the package on the wooden picnic table he'd set up underneath a shady pecan tree, and using the miniature box cutter on his key ring, sliced into the box.

"Yes," Trey said, lifting the chrome pipes from their cushioned packaging.

A Flowmaster American Thunder Header dual rear exhaust system. The missing component to the '69 Chevy Camaro he'd rescued from a junkyard near Beaumont. It currently resided in Decker's auto body shop, where he'd started working at sixteen. Decker had been dead for a few years, but his son, Corey was back in Gauthier and had been happy to give Trey the keys to the place where he'd first learned to fix cars.

If he closed his eyes, he could hear the

rumble this car would make, feel the power pulse through him as he tore up the deserted roads he used to race as a kid.

But not today.

"Dammit."

He carefully set the pipes back inside the box and cursed this being a grown-up shit to hell. Sometimes, being a grown-up sucked.

Trey carried the box inside and placed it on the floor of the Bluebird's lone closet where it would have to sit until he had time to get back to working on the Camaro. Grabbing a beer from the fridge, he unplugged his laptop and brought it outside with him to the picnic table. He straddled the wooden bench and pulled up the estimate he'd spent most of the night working on for Kiera's food truck.

She'd already secured a good portion of the equipment he would need to renovate the truck, but she didn't have any of the materials for the walls, heating system, or insulation. For a truck that size, those supplies would run her a pretty penny.

Trey had yet to list his labor cost. He wasn't sure if there would *be* any labor cost. What if Kiera took one look at the estimate and decided she couldn't afford to do the renovation? He couldn't let that happen, not after seeing how important this food truck was to her.

Hell, she'd hired *him*. If that didn't attest to how much this meant to her, Trey didn't know what did.

He decided last night that, no matter what it took, Kiera's Kickin' Kajun food truck would be up and running by the start of the shrimp festival. He would make this happen for her.

He tried her cell twice, but both times it went to voicemail. He pulled the business card she'd given him from his wallet, grinning at the mocha-skinned caricature wearing a blue polka dot apron and white chef's hat. The cartoon had big, brown eyes and held a rolling pin with *Catering by Kiera* scrolled across it. Trey dialed the business's landline.

"Catering by Kiera," a woman answered. Whoever she was, she wasn't Kiera. Her voice was too high-pitched.

"Hello," he said. "Can I speak to Kiera Coleman, please?"

"Give me a sec. I'll see if she's free."

Trey sipped his beer while he waited.

A minute later, he heard, "This is Kiera."

Now *this* smooth, ridiculously sexy voice belonged to his Kiera. She'd had that rich, sultry voice even as an innocent high schooler.

"Hey, Slim."

"Would you please stop calling me that? It's not professional."

"I'll try, but I can't make any promises. I'm so used to calling you Slim, I sometimes forget what your real name is."

She sighed. "What am I going to do with

you?"

Her question triggered a carnal ache deep within his belly. It quickly spread lower, and Trey had to fight the urge to tell her exactly what he wanted her to do with him.

Instead, he said, "I've got that estimate for you. I can swing by your kitchen and quickly talk you through it. It'll only take a few minutes."

"No," she said. "Don't come here. You'll just distract me."

A grin tugged at his lips. "I don't know about you, but that sounds like a good thing to me. I like the thought of being a distraction."

"Trey," she said in a warning tone.

He drew in a deep breath and released it with a groan.

"Yes, I know. I'm not being professional," he said. "But be realistic, Slim. You have to know it isn't easy for me to think of you in a strictly professional way."

The brief pause over the phone line made Trey think that maybe she was going to say that she couldn't either.

His spirits were crushed when she said, "Then you'll need to try harder. If you don't think you can handle it, there's still time for me to find someone else to work on the truck."

"No, don't fire me," Trey said. "I've got some great ideas for your truck. Why don't I meet you at the food truck later? I promise no funny business, just *business* business."

"Yeah, yeah. Whatever you say, Roland."

"Oh, using my first name," Trey said in a pained voice. "That's the lowest blow in the history of low blows."

She laughed. "I'll see you in a few hours. And, Trey, thanks for getting the estimate done so quickly. I really appreciate it."

"My pleasure, Slim. I'll see you later."

He ended the call, shaking his head and wondering just how long it would take him to wipe the stupid grin from his face. Kiera had always been able to wrangle a smile from him. The darker his mood, the harder she would try to drag him out of it.

When he thought of some of the things she would do to brighten his mood…

Trey closed his eyes tight and sucked in a deep breath.

Damn, but he missed that. He'd missed *her*.

He had to be the luckiest bastard in the world to be given the chance he'd been given with Kiera. He just had to convince her that he was worth another chance.

Kiera scanned the spreadsheet she'd printed from her computer, hoping she'd missed something. But she knew she hadn't. They were barely in the black this month, due in no small part to a rapid hike in oyster prices after the harvest season had produced a smaller than normal yield. She'd tried to pad her prices enough to cover shifts in market prices, but she hadn't been able to do much about the oyster issue. And, of course, eight of the ten large events she'd catered this month had her chargrilled oysters on the menu.

"It's a good thing shrimp are cheaper than usual," she muttered.

She'd probably gone through fifty pounds of shrimp trying to perfect the recipe she'd settled on for the festival.

It'll be worth it, Kiera told herself for the umpteenth time.

She didn't even have to win the top prize—although she really, *really* wanted to win that $25,000. Just the exposure that being a finalist would bring to her business would be worth the massive amount of Shrimp Napoleon wraps she and Macy had consumed over the past two weeks.

The familiar chime indicating that she had an incoming text message rang from her cellphone. Kiera grabbed the phone from her purse.

The most recent message was from Mychal: *Still waiting on that call.*

Kiera grimaced. She *had* promised to return his call from this morning. That was before she'd accidently dumped an entire container of cayenne pepper in her seafood gumbo and had to make an emergency run to the grocery store.

Her phone chimed again with another text from Mychal: *If you don't call back, I will think something is wrong.*

Kiera quickly called him.

"It's about damn time, Sunshine," Mychal answered. "I was about to swing by the house and grab Naomi so we could drive out to Louisiana to rescue you."

"You leave that lovely wife of yours where she is," Kiera said. "She's in no condition for a six-hour road trip."

"She's in no condition for a six *minute* road trip. She told me if I ever put her in the position of being eight months pregnant in August again I will lose a certain…ah…appendage."

"Ouch." Kiera laughed. "I'm going to have to come out there to see her once the baby is born."

"You need to come out here now so I can give you a first-hand demonstration of how to run a food truck," Mychal said. "It's a lot different than a regular kitchen."

"I'll think about it," she said, although Kiera knew there was no way she would make it to Austin anytime soon.

"Speaking of the truck, how is it going?" Mychal asked. "You talk to Trey Watson yet?"

"I did," Kiera said. "I was impressed. I'm meeting with him today to go over the estimate."

"I told you this guy was awesome, didn't I? Once he gets started, he's like a machine. I swear every time I checked in on the progress he had something else that I thought would take a week to finish done in a day. It's as if he has magic elves working with him or something."

"He's going to need some magic to get this truck done in time, but after seeing his work first-hand, I think he's the one. Thanks again for recommending him."

She'd debated telling Mychal about her past with Trey, but that was back when she was trying to come up with an excuse *not* to hire him. After seeing what he'd been able to do to the inside of a fifty-year-old school bus, she didn't want anyone *but* Trey working on her food truck.

"Happy I could help," Mychal said. "Just make sure you keep that truck east of the Texas state line. I'm still bitter about you always besting me in class. I don't want you moving into my territory and stealing away all my customers."

Kiera laughed as she disconnected the call and slipped the phone in her pocket. She sat at her desk for a few minutes, staring at the Disney Princesses wall calendar tacked to her wall. There were twenty-nine days before the Louisiana Shrimp Festival, only five more before the recipes for the cook-off were due to the committee.

She knew hiring Trey for this job would be like walking into the lion's den, but there was too much riding on this for her to back down now. She needed to suck it up, and just keep her head about her when she was around him.

Yeah, because that was *sooo* easy to do.

She ran both hands down her face. "Lord, just don't let me fall *too* hard again."

She pushed away from her desk, grabbed her shoulder bag from the wall peg where she hung it every morning and hit the light switch on her way out of the office.

"Macy, I'm going over to meet with the guy who's renovating the truck. I should be back in about an hour or so. Remember to make sure the cap is screwed tight on all the spices before you use them. I'm speaking from experience here."

"Will do," Macy called, not bothering to lift her head as she methodically filled halved egg whites with deviled egg mixture.

Kiera climbed into her Mazda CX-5 and headed in the direction of Trey's house, or bus, or whatever he called where he lived. She had to admit that it was a rather cool set-up, and square-footage-wise, probably not all that much smaller than her condo.

She was able to bypass some of the afternoon traffic that was a byproduct of the rapid growth spurt Maplesville had undergone in the last few years, but it still took her nearly twenty minutes to reach the edge of town where Trey lived.

Kiera tried not to allow being back here to affect her, but nostalgia won out as the memories the old sites summoned sent a wave of longing crashing through her. How many times had she and Trey parked behind that old abandoned Phillips 66 filling station to do things that could have gotten them arrested for public indecency if anyone had happened upon them? They had taken so many crazy risks.

And it hadn't always been Trey's idea.

On numerous occasions *she* had been the one to talk Trey into some of their more deliciously sinful escapades. Skinny-dipping in Ponderosa Pond, the countless quickies in the lot behind Decker's garage, the blowjob on the Ferris wheel at the St. Mary's Catholic Church fair—all her idea.

Kiera's cheeks flamed so hot she had to glance in the rearview mirror to make sure they weren't on fire.

Mason had spent so much energy sheltering her from boys like Trey, but it had only made him more intriguing and had made Kiera that much more susceptible to his sweet talk.

And, good Lord, could Trey talk a sweet game when he put his mind to it.

That's why she had to be overly cautious around him now, because after less than an hour in his presence yesterday, Kiera had felt way too many of those same feelings that had pulled her in all those years ago.

She turned onto the dirt and gravel road leading to his bus, and a few minutes later pulled in behind his pick-up truck. She walked over to the Bluebird and gave the door two sharp raps.

"Trey, it's Kiera."

The door opened…and Kiera received the shock of her life.

"Kiera!" Trey stepped in front of his thirteen-year-old daughter, Rachel, who'd answered the door while he was in the bathroom, despite the fact that he'd told her just minutes ago *not* to answer the door for any reason. "What are you doing here? I thought we were meeting at the food truck?"

"I finished up earlier than I expected." She motioned to the bus. "I would ask if I have the wrong house, but there's pretty much zero chance of that."

Trey gripped Rachel's shoulders and steered her toward the back of the bus. "Go help your brother with the dishes."

He turned back to a wide-eyed Kiera.

"Her brother? Trey Watson is the father of *two*?"

He passed another glance at the kids before

stepping outside and joining Kiera. He walked several yards from the Bluebird before finally speaking.

"Twins," Trey said. "Rachel and Roland Jr."

Kiera's mouth opened, but no words came out. She shook her head, glanced toward the bus, then back at him. "What can I say? I'm speechless." But she quickly asked, "I'm assuming they have a mother somewhere?"

Apparently, she wasn't all that speechless.

"Her name is Angie," Trey said. "She and her husband moved to Baton Rouge last month. That's one of the added bonuses of working on your truck for the next few weeks. I'll be close to my kids."

"So, you and Angie? You were married?"

He nodded. "She and I have been divorced for about…I guess it's going on three years now. We were married for a little over ten." He could practically see her mentally counting back the years.

Yes, he'd married Angie not even a year after he and Kiera broke up. It was a reckless decision on his part the same night of his break up with Kiera that was the catalyst to his marriage to Angie. A decision that had resulted in the two kids currently cleaning up the dishes they'd dirtied preparing dinner.

"So, your twins. They're what? Ten? Eleven?"

"Their thirteen."

Her chest expanded with the breath she sucked in.

If their situations were reversed Trey didn't know what he would be thinking right now, probably that he was a no-good bastard. It was pretty much the truth.

Kiera folded her arms over her chest and took a couple of steps back. Her throat worked as she swallowed several times. When she finally spoke the words came out hoarse. "Are they the reason you left?"

"No," Trey said. "I didn't meet Angie until after—"

She held her hand up. "That's all I need to know."

"Kiera—"

"No, really," she said. "That's really all I want to know."

"Come on, Slim. You just found out I have two kids and you don't want to know anything else? Do you know how hard it's been for me not to ask about your past, like whether or not you and Mychal Dickerson were an item?"

"That's none of your business," she said.

"I know it isn't; doesn't mean I still don't want to know." He closed the distance between them and lowered his head so that he could look her in the eyes. "That's why I think you're not being totally honest when you say you don't want to know anything else about *my* past."

She looked over at the picnic table, then at

the Bluebird, anywhere but at him. Finally, she returned her gaze to his.

"I'd be lying if I said I never thought about you in all these years. You were my first…my first everything. How could I *not* think about you every now and then?"

"You never tried to contact me."

"You were the one who left."

"Slim—"

"A part of me wanted to know where you were living," she continued. "How you were doing, whether or not you were in jail."

A grin tugged at the corner of his mouth. "Believe it or not, I managed to stay out of jail. Haven't gotten so much as a speeding ticket since that drag race."

Her brows arched. "If you want to give half the people in Maplesville a heart attack, lay that one on them."

"I doubt anyone would believe me."

"Probably not," she said with a soft laugh. She looked over at him, a combination of wonder and amusement in her eyes. "Of all the scenarios that played around in my head, happily married with two kids was never one of them."

"I never said I was happy." The admission slipped out before he could stop it.

Their gazes locked for a long moment. He watched as she opened her mouth then closed it, pulling her bottom lip between her teeth. Trey took a couple of steps forward, putting him just a few, tiny inches away from her. Her lips glistened, inviting him to taste them.

Trey leaned toward her, and she pulled back.

"And that's none of *my* business," Kiera finally said, turning away. Then she looked back at him. "Unless you want to share?"

Dammit. Trey ran a hand down his face and released a heavy breath. This wasn't the conversation he thought he would be having with Kiera just twenty-four hours after they'd reconnected. He knew his marriage would eventually come up, but already?

He rubbed the back of his neck.

"The one thing I don't want to do right now is recount every shitty part of my past," Trey said. "I'm not proud of the person I used to be. I was a bastard of a husband, and while I did work my ass off providing for my family, I wasn't there for them. Not the way I should have been. But I'm trying to change." He pointed to the Bluebird. "Those two kids in there mean everything to me. Every single thing I do these days is to help me become a better father for them."

"And how's that going?" she asked.

He hunched his shoulders. "I'm a work in progress."

Her eyes softened and a gentle smile touched her lips. "You're a grown-up," she said.

"Trey Watson, a responsible adult. Who would have ever imagined such a thing was possible?"

"I'm no Boy Scout, Kiera."

"You were never a Boy Scout. Even if some scout leader was foolish enough to let you join, he would have kicked you out the minute you pulled out the cigarettes and dice."

That wrung a laugh from him. "I haven't smoked a cigarette in years, either. As for the dice, well, a guy is entitled to a bit of fun every now and then, right?"

She laughed, the sound floating on the air, wrapping itself around him and warming his skin. He'd missed that laugh more than he realized. He couldn't put into words how good it felt to have her in his life again, even if it was in a strictly professional capacity.

For now.

She continued to stare at him with that subtle hint of humor lighting her eyes. It reminded Trey of the times when they were together, when she would tease him while they were out in public by sending him secret little smiles and whispering naughty things in his ear to get him riled up. Her plan usually backfired. She would make herself just as hot for him; forcing them to find a hidden place where they would attack each other like mad.

The chemistry between them had been combustible.

As he stared into her eyes, Trey could feel it

pulsing around them, stirring up feelings that had always been there, lingering just beneath the surface.

He reached for her, but she stepped away. Again.

Dammit.

"So," she said, rubbing her hands up and down her arms as if this were North Dakota in February instead of Louisiana in August. "About that estimate?"

"Yeah," Trey let out. That's why they were here, wasn't it?

He walked over to his pick-up and grabbed the estimate from where he'd tucked it when he thought he was meeting her at the food truck. Trey motioned for her to have a seat at the picnic table, then walked her through the estimate.

Kiera pointed to the column for labor cost. "This seems well below what's considered standard."

"It's the friends and family discount," Trey said.

Her eyes snapped to his. "I don't want you doing me any favors, Trey."

"Why not?"

"Because favors tend to come with strings attached."

"I wouldn't—"

"That's just one part of it," she said, cutting him off. "Look, Trey, I want to do this on my own. I *need* to do this on my own. For once in my life I need to know that I made something happen, without someone else coming to my rescue."

Trey put both hands up. "Fine," he said. "I'll revise my labor cost. That'll add another twenty percent to the bottom line. Is that doable?"

She stared at the printout for several moments before she slowly nodded. She looked up at him and her eyes were once again sparkling.

"Yes," she said, awe coloring her voice. "That's doable. This is going to happen. Kiera's Kickin' Kajun will be a reality."

The joy on her face was infectious.

"Congratulations," Trey said.

His gaze dipped to her lips, which she nervously wetted with a swipe of her tongue. It made them glisten once again and, this time, there was not a damn thing on the face of the planet that could stop Trey from tasting them.

"Daddy?"

Except for that.

Trey's eyes shut briefly before he turned to the Bluebird, where Rachel was hanging out the open door.

"What is it, Rach?"

"RJ is keeping the remote from me and it's my turn to watch TV."

Trey kneaded the bridge of his nose. He looked over at Kiera and grimaced. "Did I mention that raising kids isn't necessarily the easiest job in the world?"

Kiera folded her arms over her chest and grinned. "I want to see how you're going to tackle this one, Daddy."

He let out a groan. "You know when you say the word *daddy* it has an entirely different meaning, right?"

She leveled him the censorious look that statement deserved, but ruined it by bursting out laughing. She was so beautiful when she laughed. It lit up her entire face.

"Damn, it's good to see you again, Slim."

Her eyes still sparkling with her smile, she said in a soft voice, "I never thought I'd ever say this, but it's good to see you, too, Trey."

The door opened again.

"Daddy!" Rachel yelled.

"In a minute," Trey called. "I guess I need to handle this." He tipped his head toward the bus. "You want to come in for a minute?"

A shadow passed over Kiera's face before she bolted up from the picnic table. "No." She shook her head. "I should go." She grabbed the estimate and started for her car. She tossed a look over her shoulder. "Let me know if you need anything before you get started on the truck."

Trey stared at her SUV as she executed a quick three-point turn and took off, the back tires kicking up dust as she sprinted away.

Chapter Four

Trey wedged the blade of the tile scraper between the scuffed vinyl tile and the subfloor of the truck. He didn't know what kind of adhesive they'd used to lay the tile, but he could glue Humpty Dumpty back together again with this shit. He had to put all of his weight behind every shove.

When working a job he always built in a little extra time for snafus, but Trey tried to save that for last minute issues that tended to pop up. He was only five days into this renovation and these stubborn floor tiles were already eating away any padding he'd added to his schedule.

What had Kiera been thinking, buying such a heap of junk? And what unscrupulous bastard had pocketed twenty grand for this?

More than once since he'd begun stripping out the truck's interior he'd had to stop himself from asking Kiera for a name. He didn't like the idea of anyone being taken for a ride, but the thought of someone taking advantage of Kiera?

His fingers flexed around the handle of the scraper.

Anger fueled him through another four square feet of tile removal. He gathered the loose tiles and tossed them into the bed of his truck. He'd dump them at the old scrapyard on his way home.

Trey was well into his work groove when an unexpected find stopped him dead in his tracks. He lifted up a bit more of the tile and encountered the ground, littered with maple leaves and pine needles, below.

"Son of a bitch."

This was way more than just a snafu.

Trey jumped into his truck, driving first to the dumpster to unload the broken tiles before heading to Kiera's. As he drove east toward the side of town where her catering company was located, he scarfed down the lunch he'd packed that morning.

Trey veered off the exit his navigation system instructed him to take, then did a couple of right and left turns before the corrugated building with the Catering by Kiera sign came into view. The surge of pride that filled his chest expanded even more when he pulled up alongside the building and saw just how big it was. It wasn't just that she'd managed to accomplish something of this magnitude; he was proud that she'd found the courage to take it on at all.

He still remembered the argument they'd had when she'd told him she was going to the University of New Orleans instead of culinary school. Trey had instantly suspected that her brother had been the driving force behind her decision. Mason had hounded her about getting a traditional four-year degree, because it's what their father would have wanted.

Only an asshole would use a girl's dead dad to try to control her.

Maplesville wasn't that big of a town, but Trey would do his best to avoid running into Mason Coleman while he was here. He and Mason had gone through twelve years of school together without incident, but all that had changed once Trey started dating the guy's baby sister. Trey automatically became Enemy Number One. And one surefire way *not* to land himself back in Kiera's good graces was to get into a confrontation with her brother.

The minute he entered Kiera's building Trey was bombarded with a barrage of aromas that made his stomach growl. The small lobby was empty, so he ventured further, going through a door that led to a large, open kitchen.

A woman with bright blue hair greeted him. "Hey there. Nice tat," she said, nodding toward his arm.

Trey nodded back. "Nothing compared to those full sleeves of yours. Great ink. I'm Trey, by the way, the guy renovating Kiera's food truck."

"Macy." She ground the palm of her flour-covered hand into a mound of dough.

"This place smells phenomenal. What are

you making?"

"Brioche. It's for our homemade bread pudding. But it's probably the Turducken you smell: turkey, stuffed with duck, that's stuffed with chicken. We served it at the city council meeting last week and it was a huge hit, so now it's what everyone around here wants."

"I can see why. Make that *smell* why."

"Stick around for the cornbread and pork sausage dressing that's also stuffed inside of it. *That's* when you'll smell phenomenal. One of Kiera's specialties."

"Is she around?"

Macy motioned her head again. "Through the swing doors. You can't miss her."

Trey walked through the swinging doors and found Kiera hunched over a platter. She looked up at him, her forehead creasing with her frown. "What are you doing here?"

"Hopefully, I'm sampling some of that food."

A hint of a smile tipped up her lips. "You stopped in the middle of working on my truck and drove all the way across town just to beg for food? Did we not discuss the time crunch we're under?"

"Yeah, but I ran into an issue with the truck, one that needed addressing right away."

The frown returned. "What's wrong?"

"There's a part of the floor that's completely rotted out," Trey answered.

Her eyes slid closed. She brought both hands up and started rubbing her temples. "I don't need this kind of headache."

"Nobody needs this kind of headache, Slim, but shit happens. When tackling a project this big, nine times out of ten you're going to encounter something you weren't planning for."

"The truck itself was supposed to be my 'Shit Happens' moment."

He grinned. "Sometimes, if you're really special, you get to have more than one."

"Don't laugh at me, Trey."

"I'm not laughing at you."

"You're not laughing *with* me, because I'm not laughing."

He swallowed the laugh that tried to escape and put both hands on her shoulders. "It'll be okay, Slim. As far as setbacks go, this one isn't all that bad."

"Except that this month's budget has absolutely no room for a new floor for that money pit of a truck," she said. "What am I looking at, time- and money-wise?"

"Believe it or not, this may be a blessing in disguise. Instead of spending so much time trying to lift up those tiles, I can just take a sledgehammer to the floor. See, sometimes when shit happens, it turns out to be a good thing."

She blew out an aggravated sigh. The annoyed look she shot his way wrestled another chuckle from him.

"What about the cost?" she asked.

"Don't worry about that right now."

"I need to know if I can afford this, or if I'll have to hold off on getting the truck renovated."

Trey shook his head. "That's not the way I operate. Once I start a job, I don't stop until it's complete. This truck will get done, even if you have to pay the balance off in installments. My clients do that all the time."

"I'll feel better if you can give me a ballpark estimate," she said. "I'd rather have the renovation paid in full at the end of the month, but if it does turn out that I need to pay it off in installments, I want to know how much I have to budget."

Damn, she was stubborn. Stubborn and sexy-as-hell. Especially with that smudge of flour dusting her cheek.

"It'll be another eight-hundred," Trey said, throwing out the first number that came to his head. He figured anything under a thousand wouldn't be enough to force her to halt work on the truck.

Honestly, he didn't know how much the materials for the new flooring would cost, but Trey had already decided that he would absorb the cost. He would also find a way to cut the eight hundred dollars from the final cost of the renovation. This job wasn't about making money; it was about making Kiera's dreams come true.

He shouldn't have even bothered telling her about the floor, but he'd wanted an excuse to see her. It had been several days since he'd seen her, and even then it was only for a quick meeting to go over the blueprints he'd drawn up.

"I can handle eight hundred," Kiera said.

"Good. Now that we've taken care of that, how about serving me up a plate of whatever it is you're fixing over there? It's been a while since I've been your guinea pig."

Her mouth twitched with a grin as she walked around to the other side of the stainless steel table and picked up one of the narrow, rectangular plates.

"This is what I'm entering into the Louisiana Shrimp Festival's Cook-Off. The submission is due by five o'clock today. I've got three samples, each with subtle adjustments to the recipe. Let me know which one you like the best." She handed him a glass. "Sip this between each sample to cleanse your palate."

Trey tested each sample, then pointed to the middle portion. "I like this one the best. It has just a hint of lemon, right? The acid is a nice compliment to the shrimp."

Her eyes widened.

"What?" he asked. "I like to watch the occasional cooking show. You absorb a few things."

"Trey Watson, you couldn't boil an egg back when I knew you."

He shrugged. "Yeah, well, bachelorhood will force you to do some scary things, like cooking. Fast food every night gets expensive." Inspiration struck him like a slap behind the head. He immediately jumped on the idea. "Maybe I should cook for you some time."

Her expression turned wary. "I don't think that's a good idea."

"Sure it is." He rounded the table and came to stand in front of her. "Come on. Let me make up for all those times you used to steal your mom's car to bring me a hot meal when I was working at Decker's."

"I never stole my mother's car," Kiera said, taking a step back. "I would borrow it."

"Without permission," Trey added, closing the distance between them again. "In most parts of the world they call that stealing."

"You would know," she said with a nervous chuckle, backing up until she butted against the stainless steel table.

Slowly shaking his head, Trey braced his palms flat on the table on either side of her, hemming her in. He stared into her eyes and allowed all the need that had been building over the past five days, since the moment they nearly kissed outside his house, to shine through.

His voice rough with want, Trey said, "You know damn well I never took anything that wasn't freely given to me, Slim."

Kiera's eyes dropped to his mouth as her own lips parted slightly. She could feel his warm breath against her skin, the sensation causing need to pool deep in her belly.

Trey edged forward and traced his mouth lightly along her jawline. "I dare you to deny it," he murmured against her skin.

"I...I can't," she said, her voice a husky whisper.

"I know you can't," he breathed. "Because, back then, there was nothing you used to love more than giving it to me."

He skimmed a path from her ear, down her cheek, to the edge of her lips. His feather light touch teased her sensitive nerve-endings, triggering a deluge of tingles to cascade along her skin. He brought his hand up and captured her head, slipping his fingers into her hair and gently turning her face to him. As he closed in on her mouth, a blend of remembered longing and deep carnal need swirled inside of her.

This was Trey. *Her* Trey.

The first man she'd truly loved, the *only* man she'd truly loved. She'd ached with yearning for him for so long; hoping, wishing, praying that one day, by some miracle, she would taste his lips again.

The moment she did, everything else in her world ceased to exist.

He was everything. All that she wanted. All she ever needed.

The thought both scared her and excited her. Kiera knew the danger of falling under his spell again, but right now, she didn't care. Right now, all she wanted to do was experience Trey. The taste, the texture, everything about his kiss brought her back to a time when the man holding her in his arms was hers and hers alone.

Whatever morsel of resistance that dared to remain was abandoned when Trey finally laid full claim to her, pushing past the seam of her lips and finding his way inside. His warm, soft tongue brushed across hers before he sucked it inside of his mouth.

God, he tasted just as she remembered, sweet and spicy and deliciously intoxicating.

Her hands came around him and traveled up his back, to his head. Kiera held him there, crushing him to her. There was something instinctual about needing to feel him wedged between her thighs, a primal impulse that demanded it. Her legs parted and she pulled him against her. The second Trey positioned his body flush against hers, instinct took over.

He gripped her hips and held tight. Kiera's mind went numb at the feel of his hardness pressed against her pulsing center. She drove her tongue into his mouth over and over again; the need to have him—all of him—was so intense her limbs shook with it.

Kiera locked her right leg behind his left knee. She flattened her palms on his backside and clutched him, her fingernails impaling him through his jeans.

Trey picked her up, turned her around…and crashed right into a cart of utensils. Spoons, tongs, and several extremely sharp knives fell to the floor.

"Holy shit," Trey said, looking down at the mess on the floor.

Kiera blinked several times, trying to find her bearings after the mind-blowing kiss. She registered the sound of shoes squeaking on the linoleum flooring.

"Macy." Kiera pushed away from him just before her assistant came barging through the swinging doors.

"Is everything okay?" Macy asked.

"It's fine," Kiera said. She dropped to the scattered utensils. "Uh, these will…uh…need to be steam cleaned."

If they hadn't stopped when they had, this whole place would need to be steam cleaned.

Kiera looked up to find Macy staring at her with a shrewd tilt to her lips. Her too-perceptive-for-her-own-damn-good assistant was not fooled.

"How is the praline topping for the bread pudding coming?" Kiera asked.

"Just fine," Macy said.

"You want to get back to it?"

Macy looked as if she was on the verge of speaking, but decided against it. She simply turned and headed back through the swinging doors.

Kiera's head fell forward as her entire body went limp with relief. "That cannot happen again," she said.

Even as she said the words her brain fought back with protests. Not only did she want that to happen again, but she wanted it to happen over and over and over. Until they were both naked and barely breathing.

Kiera couldn't suppress the shudder that quaked through her.

"Maybe it shouldn't have happened here," Trey said.

"It shouldn't have happened at all." She braced her hands on her thighs and pushed herself up. "From the minute I decided to hire you I promised myself I would not let being around you affect me."

"I hate to break it to you, Slim, but you made yourself a promise you won't be able to keep. There's too much history between us."

"Oh, no. I'm keeping it," she said. She pointed a finger at him. "As long as *you* keep your word. Since when did stealing kisses in the middle of the day become acceptable professional behavior?"

"I thought we went over this already? I didn't steal anything. You could have told me to stop any time."

"You never should have started it." She cradled her head in her hands and dropped her chin to her chest. "I knew hiring you would be trouble."

Trey took her chin between his fingers and lifted her face up to his. "Trouble can be a whole lot of fun," he said. He traced the pad of his thumb along her bottom lip, which still felt bruised from their intense kiss. "Don't you remember how much fun it used to be, Slim? If you don't, there are several things I can do to jog your memory."

Another shudder went through her. In a pained voice, Kiera said, "You're not making this easy, Trey."

"What?"

"Resisting you."

"Now why would I want to make that easy for you?" he murmured against her cheek.

"Don't," she said. She flattened both palms against his chest and tried to shove him away, but she didn't put an ounce of force behind it. "I told you we weren't going to do this."

"Yeah, but you weren't very convincing, especially when you sucked my tongue into your mouth."

"Move," she said, pushing with more force this time.

Kiera prayed he'd give in, because if he tried to kiss her again, she knew she would cave.

After several intense moments where Kiera was sure he would lay claim to her mouth once again, he backed away, giving her some much needed space. He returned to the plate with her recipe samples, taking several more bites before washing it down with the citrus-flavored drink she'd given him.

Kiera gaped at him. "Seriously?"

"What?" he asked, wiping his hands on the back of his jeans.

"After all that just happened, you go back to eating?"

"I'm not letting this food go to waste."

She threw her hands up and blew out an aggravated breath. "Why would I expect anything different from you?"

"Hey, you're the one who put the breaks on," he said. "If I had to choose between finishing what we started and finishing the food, this shrimp stuff isn't what I would be eating right now, but you took that choice out of my hands."

Heat engulfed her as his words conjured an image that had Kiera needing a cold shower this very instant. She cursed her body's reaction to him.

Dammit, she knew better than this. She couldn't allow herself to be swept away by his decadent kisses, because once he was done with the renovation and hightailed it away from Maplesville again, she would be left trying to recover from the whirlwind that was Trey Watson.

"I've got work to do," Kiera said, spinning around and marching in the direction of the industrial coolers. She yanked hard on the door and cursed again when she felt her shoulder twinge. Injuring herself would be the icing on the cake.

"I'm not going to apologize for kissing you," Trey said from just a few feet behind her. "Because I'm sure as hell not sorry about it. But I shouldn't have crossed that line, especially after promising you I wouldn't."

Her head fell forward. "I shouldn't have let you," she whispered.

But she did.

Not only had she let him cross that line, she'd been just as into that kiss as he was. Kiera could deny it all she wanted to, but her body had resonated with want with every thrust of his tongue. She still wanted him. Badly.

There was a knock on the door just before it swung open. Macy peeked inside.

"Kiera, the warehouse just called. The deep fryer is in. Are you still planning to drive out to Slidell to get it, or do you want them to deliver it? There's an extra charge."

"I can pick it up," Trey said. "I have to go out there to buy the materials for the floors." He paused for a second before he said, "But you should come with me. I need your input on the light fixtures."

"I…I can't…" *Be in the same car with you.* "I can't leave Macy to handle prepping for tonight's catering job on her own."

"Oh, I forgot to tell you," Macy said. "Tiana and Nicholas are both coming in early. There was a busted water main near Delgado's campus, so all the culinary school's afternoon classes were cancelled. We can handle tonight's job."

Kiera turned back to Trey.

He held his hands up. "You're the one on the tight deadline."

"He's right," Macy called as she backed out of the doorway. "Think Kiera's Kickin' Kajun."

Unease coursed down Kiera's spine, but she couldn't come up with a plausible excuse not to join him. "Let me get my purse."

The grin that formed on Trey's lips kicked her trepidation into high gear. "I'll meet you at my truck."

In the two minutes it took to grab her purse from her office, Kiera contemplated following Trey in her own car at least a half dozen times. Being confined in a small space with that man for thirty-five minutes had trouble written all over it. And after the brief taste of trouble she'd just had, she doubted she had the will to resist him for much longer.

No other man had *ever* affected her the way he had. And still did.

She walked outside and stopped short.

Good Lord. Sometimes one just had to take a step back and give gorgeousness its due.

Trey stood just outside the open passenger door of his truck, talking on his cellphone. He'd slipped on dark aviator sunglasses, which only made him a thousand times hotter. He looked downright edible, his brown skin even and flawless, a five o'clock shadow making its presence known even though it wasn't even two o'clock yet.

He was all hard planes and defined sinew. She remembered just what it felt like to have those arms, corded with well-honed muscles, wrapped around her; to have his lean, powerful hips wedged between her thighs as his hard body drove deep.

God, but she wanted him.

God, but she was stupid.

And a glutton for punishment. And horny as hell.

The only man she'd slept with in the past year was Garrett, and that selfish bastard wouldn't care if she came even if she begged him for it, which she'd often had to do. Not as if it ever made a difference.

Trey would care.

That was yet another thing she remembered

all too well. It didn't matter if it was a five-minute quickie in the cab of his dad's old truck, or hours of making love in his bed. Trey had always made certain her needs were met before he even thought about finding his own release.

Kiera was suddenly gripped with a yearning so deep, so strong, she ached with it. Why did something that had been so good have to end so badly?

"Are you ready?" Trey called, pocketing his cellphone.

Willing those remembered urges to remain right where she'd left them—in the past—she nodded and continued for his truck.

"The lumber yard has everything I need in stock." He stepped aside so she could climb into the passenger seat. "They're getting the order together now. It'll be ready to load into my truck by the time we get there."

"Will my fryer fit?" Kiera asked.

"It should fit in the rear of the cab, but if it doesn't I can drive back to Slidell for it. I just found out that my night is free." She looked at him with a raised brow. "I was supposed to have the kids, but Donald's company has some kind of movie night thing. I can't compete with a movie and free popcorn."

"Donald?"

"My ex Angie's new husband." He shut her door and rounded the truck. After slipping behind the wheel, he turned the radio to a sports talk station before pulling onto the roadway.

Kiera had been fighting the urge to ask about his ex-wife all week. She'd told him she didn't want to know more, and at the time, she didn't, but lately, all she could think about was the woman who had managed to turn the baddest of bad boys into a responsible adult.

After several minutes, Kiera couldn't take it anymore. She dialed down the volume on the radio and turned slightly in her seat.

"Tell me about Angie." Okay, not as subtle as she was going for.

Trey glanced her way. "What do you want to know?"

Why was she good enough to marry and not me?

"Just…you know…stuff. When did you two meet?"

He steered one-handed while rubbing the back of his neck with the other hand.

"I can beat around the bush with a bunch of bullshit small talk, or I can give it to you straight. Your choice, Slim."

"Straight, please."

He released a ragged breath before continuing. "I met Angie at a bar in Houston. After a few minutes of talking we discovered that we'd both just suffered through one of the shittiest days of our lives, so we decided to hang out for a while."

"A misery loves company kind of thing?"

"Basically. We both had too much to drink,

went back to her place, and made the twins that very same night."

Her throat suddenly felt uncomfortably tight, probably from the jealousy and hurt lodged in there.

"Wow," she said after a beat. "You don't play around, do you?"

"I was stupid and irresponsible, but as you know, that was pretty much my mode of operation back then. I soon found out that Angie wasn't the type of girl you picked up in a bar, got pregnant, and then left high and dry." He frowned. "Actually, no girl should be that kind of girl, but back then I was only thinking about myself."

"What made Angie different from 'that kind of girl?'"

He shrugged, drumming his thumbs on the steering wheel. "She was from a good family. Her dad is a college professor, her mom was a regional director of a bank before she retired." He glanced at her. "As you can probably imagine, I wasn't exactly the kind of guy they pictured their daughter marrying. Honestly, when I asked her to marry me, I was certain she would say no."

"But she didn't."

"No, actually, she did. She turned me down more than once, because I *wasn't* the kind of guy a girl like her would ever marry. But I kept asking." He shook his head. "I don't know, I guess I was just fed up with being the guy that was never good enough."

A painful ache pierced Kiera's chest. She knew there were many people who'd made him feel that way, some of them were her own family members.

After several moments of uneasy silence, Kiera asked, "What made her eventually say yes?"

"She started getting pressure from her family. In their world, being married to a lowlife auto mechanic was better than being an unwed mother."

Kiera flinched at the bitterness in his tone.

"We tried to make it work," he continued. "But it was doomed from the start."

"You said you two were married for over ten years. Sounds as if it worked for a while."

"A testament to how much shit Angie was willing to put up with." He looked over at her. "I was a lousy husband, Kiera. I begged Angie to marry me then resented the fact that I was tied down. I couldn't tell you how many times I left her alone with the kids so I could go out with the guys, or hung around the garage after work so I wouldn't have to go home. She has every right to hate me, but she's never allowed any bad feelings she holds toward me to get between me and my kids."

She paused for a moment, then in a softer voice, asked, "Do you regret getting married?"

He glanced in the rearview mirror, then adjusted the air conditioning vents. Finally, he said, "I resented it, but I can't bring myself to regret it. If I say my marriage was a mistake, then I'm saying my children were a mistake." He shook his head. "I've done some shitty things in my life, Slim, but RJ and Rachel, they're the best two things in the world. They deserve a dad that's worthy of them."

She twisted a bit more toward him, bringing one leg up on the seat. She propped her elbow against the headrest and rested her cheek in her palm. She studied him for several moments before asking, "What makes you think you're not worthy of them?"

Trey glanced in the rearview mirror again before pulling into the right lane and passing a semi-tractor trailer.

"Things are getting better between us," he said once they were back in the left lane. "But it wasn't always that way. It took me a while to realize that there's a lot more to being a parent than just making sure your kids have food on the table and a roof over their heads. Just being a provider isn't enough. I want to actually be there for them."

Unlike his own father.

He didn't say the words, but Kiera could tell he was thinking them. By the time they started dating Trey's dad had already been dead a few years, but she had managed to get Trey to open up about their rocky relationship. The stories he'd told her about the way his dad would leave for days at a time, and how things were even worse when he *did* stick around, made Kiera appreciate the short eleven years she'd had with her own father that much more.

After a moment, she asked, "What about the twins' stepdad?"

He shrugged. "I tried not to like him, but then I realized it was a knee-jerk reaction to the fact that someone else was helping to raise my kids. Donald's a good guy. He's a better husband to Angie than I ever was, and he never tries to one-up me when it comes to the kids. It's actually a pretty good situation, probably better than I deserve."

Kiera studied him from across the cab of the truck. She'd thought of him way too much over the years, wondering what had become of him, what kind of life he was leading. His reality was so vastly different from anything she had imagined. He was no longer the hell raiser; he was a *dad*.

"I like this more mature and responsible Trey," she finally said.

A cocky smile lifted the corner of his mouth, and despite his sunglasses, she knew his eyes were sparkling with laughter just from the way they creased at the corners.

"Bet you never thought I'd come back to Maplesville a brand new man."

"Actually, I never thought you'd come back at all. When you left, I thought it was for good."

He looked over at her, soberness replacing the humor of a moment ago. "If anyone could bring me back home, Slim, it's you."

His solemnly spoken words caused a ripple of awareness to flutter through her chest and settle low in her belly.

Kiera damned that feeling to hell, yet she couldn't deny the pleasure stirring inside of her at the realization that she had the power to bring Trey back to Maplesville.

But she was also the reason he'd left in the first place. *He* left *her*. *That's* what she needed to remember.

Kiera knew she should keep her distance from him, but it was getting harder by the minute. At one time this man owned every inch of her heart, and after the kiss they'd shared back in her kitchen her stupid heart was just begging to be claimed again.

She was in *so* much trouble.

They arrived at the lumberyard, and just as was promised, there was a worker with a pallet of plywood and boards ready to load into the bed of Trey's truck.

As the lumber they'd purchased was wrapped in a blue tarp and secured with rope in the back of the truck, she picked out fluorescent light panels and listened as Trey debated the merits of adding spotlights over the prep station.

He picked up a couple of other things he needed, then they headed for the restaurant supply warehouse, which was just down the street from the lumberyard.

When they arrived, Kiera encountered her second "Shit Happens" moment of the day.

"What is this?" she asked, pointing to the fryer that was half the size of what she'd picked out. "This is supposed to be a two-basket fryer."

The salesman huddled behind his monitor and pecked at the keyboard. Kiera knew by the wrinkle that formed on his forehead that she would not like what he had to say.

"What's wrong?" she asked.

"Well, the fryer you want is now on backorder."

"How long will it take to get here?"

He pointed at the screen. "This is showing twelve weeks."

"What!" She yelled loud enough to turn the heads of several shoppers.

"Okay, Slim, let's take it down a notch." Trey wrapped an arm around her waist and drew her back a few steps. "This isn't the end of the world."

"I don't have three months to wait on a fryer. I don't have three weeks!"

He took her hands and squeezed them between his palms. "How critical is it for you to have a double basket fryer? According to the menu you showed me, you're going to be doing mostly wraps."

"Yes, but some of the ingredients will need to be fried, like the shrimps and oysters for the seafood remoulade wrap. And what about the blueprints you created? They've been drawn up with the dimensions of that specific fryer." She pointed toward the computer monitor. "The one they're trying to pawn off on me is too small. It's going to leave a huge gap."

"Actually, the one they're trying to pawn off on you might be perfect. Give me just a sec."

He took out his cellphone and brought up a calculator app. After punching in a few numbers, he turned the phone around to face her. "If I install that fryer, it's going to leave just enough space for you to get the bigger cooler you want, give or take a few inches."

Kiera looked at the phone, as if the string of numbers meant anything to her. "Are you sure?" she asked.

"I'll probably have to move everything to the right by about an inch or so, but that's no problem. I'll change the dimensions in the CAD program when I get back to the Bluebird tonight. I can make this work."

"Oh, my God. Trey that would be awesome!"

"Shhh." He dipped his head and whispered in her ear. "Don't get too excited. Pretend you're still pissed. That way they'll think you're doing them a favor when you reluctantly accept that fryer for twenty-percent off in order to make up for their snafu."

Kiera had to swallow her laugh. He'd grown up a bit, but he still had some of the old Trey in him.

By the time the salesman and store manager finished apologizing, Kiera was sure she could get whatever she wanted out of them. She and Trey also picked out the larger cooler that would work perfectly in the space that the smaller fryer would accommodate.

Back in his truck, Kiera said, "Well, that was pretty damn awesome," as she secured the seatbelt across her chest.

"That it was," Trey agreed. "I should take you shopping with me all the time. You've got some sweet negotiating skills."

"Comes with the job. Some of my produce suppliers drive a hard bargain."

"Ah, the cutthroat world of catering," Trey said as he turned out of the warehouse's parking lot.

"Whatever." She laughed. "It *is* cutthroat. It's also exhausting. It's a good thing Macy and the other two can handle tonight's job because I'm dead on my feet."

"Yet another reason you should let me cook you dinner tonight."

"Haven't we discussed this already? Having you cook me dinner wouldn't be very professional."

He pulled up to a red light and glanced at her. "There's such a thing as a business dinner."

Kiera barked out another laugh. "I'm supposed to believe you're inviting me over for a business dinner? I don't know who you think you're fooling, Trey Watson, but I know exactly what would happen if I came over to that cute little bus of yours for dinner."

Trey closed his eyes. "Tell me what you think would happen, Slim. Talk slow."

She slapped his arm. "A lot about you has changed, but you're still the same in so many ways."

He looked over at her and with a smile that was as cocky as it was devastating, said, "In the best ways, sweetheart. I'm still the same in all the best ways."

Chapter Five

Kiera pulled up next to Trey's quad cab, which he'd parked underneath a tree on the very edge of the industrial park. The driver's side door was open and a heated discussion between two radio personalities over a bad call in the Saints pre-season football game last night streamed out from the speakers.

She spent all of last week working on a huge catering job for the Washington Parish School Board, who had hired Catering by Kiera to provide special back-to-school lunches for the faculty and staff at all ten of the parish's public schools. Even though they'd broken the job up into two schools per day, it had still kept Kiera too busy to check on the food truck's progress.

"Trey?" she called as she bypassed sheets of metal stacked a few feet away from her food truck. She walked up to the back of the truck and her mouth fell open.

"Oh, my God! Are you kidding me?"

The inside of the truck gleamed with a shiny new aluminum floor and ceiling. Most of the walls were covered in the aluminum as well, with the exception of a small portion on the left side.

"Hey," Trey called from deep inside the

truck. "Give me just a minute."

Using a powered nail gun, he secured the aluminum sheet onto the wall then set the nail gun on the floor. He walked toward the rear of the truck, that ever-present smile on his face.

"How's it going, Slim?"

"Based on what I see here, it's going fantastic," Kiera answered. She accepted the hand he held out for her. "I can't believe how much you've gotten done. You're like a machine."

"Once I start a project I just really get into it," he said. "The electrician finished up with his wiring yesterday and I went to work. I did hire someone to help with the ceiling," he said. "He'll be back to help finish off the plumbing, too, once we get the sink in place."

"This is truly amazing," she said, turning around in the center of the truck. Goose bumps traveled along her skin as the realization that her dream was coming true began to sink in. "Who would have thought having Trey Watson back in town would turn out to be a good thing?"

He put his hand to his chest. "You really know how to flatter a guy, Slim." He snapped his fingers. "I'm happy you're here. I ran into a slight problem with the hood." He pointed to the exhaust vent hood, wrapped in plastic and leaning against the wall.

"What's wrong now?" Kiera asked, her shoulders slumping.

"The adjustments for the new fryer and cooler made the hood a few inches too big for the space. But it's nothing to get too worked up about. I've already found

someone willing to do a trade. In fact, it's a guy your buddy Mychal put me in contact with."

"Thank goodness for Mychal. That man is constantly saving my butt."

"Yeah, he seems like a good guy." Trey shifted from one foot to the other, and after a pause, asked, "Was there anything…you know…between you two?"

Kiera's mouth fell open. "I can't believe you seriously just asked me that."

Trey put his hands up. "Yeah, I know, it's none of my business. Still, I want to know."

"Men," she said with an aggravated huff. "No, there was never anything between us. We were classmates and really good friends. Mychal happens to be happily married with a baby on the way."

"I met his wife while I was working on his truck, but I didn't know if…well, you know."

Her head reared back. "You think I would date a married man?"

"No! I…" He ran a hand down his face. "I just…I was curious, that's all."

"Again, I never dated Mychal, but that doesn't mean I haven't been with anyone else since you," she tacked on.

She needed him to know that she'd picked up the pieces of the broken heart he'd left her with and moved on. Sort of.

"As much as I love the thought of being your one and only, I know the men in this town wouldn't be foolish enough to let a girl like you stay single, Slim." He reached over and brushed her hair behind her ear. "There's only one fool I know who would do something like that."

Her chest expanded with the deep breath she sucked in as she stared at his mouth. The memory of the kiss they'd shared last week came roaring back, teasing her senses and making her want to finish what they'd started in her kitchen.

"You should get back to work," Kiera said, holding on to the last dregs of her self-preservation instincts.

Trey's gaze remained on her for several intense moments before he dropped his hand and took a couple of steps back. As he returned to his work, the weight of his words remained. His admission hung in the air, heavy and heart-wrenching.

She hated him for the way he'd left, without explanation; with nothing more than a curt "this isn't going to work." But she still mourned the time they'd missed out on, the memories they could have made over the past fourteen years.

She had *wanted* to be his one and only. She'd wanted that more than anything. But he'd carelessly thrown her love away and left her with nothing but *what ifs*.

But he was back now, and a new *what if* had surfaced.

What if there was still a chance for them?

The sound of a rumbling car engine knocked Kiera out of her ruminations.

"There shouldn't be anyone back here," she said, walking to the rear of the truck.

"Oh, great," Kiera said when she spotted her brother's car pulling up next to hers. She quickly jumped out of the truck and walked over to him. Mason greeted her with a hug.

"What are you doing here?" Kiera gestured at his tailored dark-gray suit. "Why aren't you at work?"

"I had a meeting with Matthew Gauthier at his office. I stopped at your kitchen to see how things were going on the renovation and Macy told me you were here. Worked out perfectly. You can give me a tour."

She saw Mason's jaw harden and knew he'd spotted Trey. "What in the hell is *he* doing here?"

"Hello to you, too, Mason," came Trey's cool reply.

Ignoring Trey's greeting, her brother pointed to her. "Kiera, what's going on?"

"Guess there's no love for an old classmate," Trey said before Kiera could speak. He stood along side her; he and Mason eyed each other like two cobras ready to strike.

"What are you doing here?" Mason asked again.

"Trey is renovating Kiera's Kickin' Kajun," she explained.

"*This* is who you hired to work on the truck?" Her brother asked, hooking a thumb in Trey's direction. "Why are you even in Maplesville? Isn't there a bank you should be robbing somewhere?"

"Mason, stop it," Kiera said.

"Never robbed a bank," Trey remarked. "May have robbed the cradle, but never a bank."

Kiera's eyelids slid shut.

"Keep talking, asshole," Mason said, taking a menacing step forward.

"Enough Mason. You know I've been looking high and low for someone to renovate the truck. Trey came highly recommended."

"I thought you said you would call the guy Mychal used?"

"I did," she said.

Mason's mouth fell open. He ran a disgusted gaze from the top of Trey's head to his feet. "*He's* the one who did the work on Mychal's truck?"

"That's right," Trey said. "The grease monkey turned out to be good for something."

Kiera rolled her eyes. The smug look on Trey's face was not helping the situation at all.

"Yes, Trey is the one who renovated Mychal's truck," she said. "And he came all the way from Houston to work on mine."

"I don't care if you built the damn space shuttle," Mason said to Trey. "I don't want you working on this truck, and I sure as hell don't want you around Kiera."

Trey braced his feet apart and folded his arms over his chest. That tight smile still in place, he said, "Well, that's too bad, because I'm already working on this truck, and because it happens to be Kiera's truck, I'll have to be around her a whole lot. I guess you'll just have to deal with it."

"I don't have to deal with shit," her brother spat.

"Oh, that's right. You've never been good at dealing with stuff. After all this time, just look at how pissed off you still are about the fact that I dated your little sister."

"I was pissed about you banging my little sister."

"Mason!"

"Yeah, I did that, too," Trey said. "A lot."

"Trey!" Kiera said.

"I should kick your ass right now," Mason growled between clenched teeth.

Kiera wedged herself between them before Mason's balled fist found its mark. This pissing match between the two of them had gone on long enough—fourteen years too long.

"If you two don't stop acting like I'm not even here, I'm going to kick both of your asses," she said.

Trey backed off, but her stubborn-as-hell brother didn't take the hint. He pointed a finger at Trey.

"Pack up your shit and get out of here. You're fired," Mason said. "*I'll* hire someone to work on the truck." He looked over at Kiera. "The place I found in Philadelphia can do it. I'll hire someone to drive it up there if I have to."

"No, Mason. I need the truck done by the end of the month. I don't have time to have it driven to and from Philadelphia. And even if I did, the answer is still no. This is *my* truck. It's *my* business, and it was *my* decision to hire Trey."

"Oh yeah?" he said. "Well, you wouldn't have this truck if I hadn't given you the money for it."

Kiera stepped back as if he'd slapped her in the face. And that's exactly how it felt.

"I knew it," she said, her teeth clenched so hard she could barely get the words out.

"Shit," Mason cursed.

"You stepped in it now, bro," Trey said.

Mason jabbed a finger at him. "Shut the fuck up."

"Why don't you *both* shut up," Kiera said.

She turned her back on them both and marched toward the row of silver maple trees that defined the property line.

"Come back here," her brother ordered, but she continued her march.

She stopped just before the trees, but refused to turn around even after the sound of his footsteps crunching the leaves stopped.

"I'm sorry," Mason said.

She whipped around. "I knew I never should have taken that money from you. But you don't have to worry; I'll pay you back. Every damn penny, interest included."

"Kiera, stop it."

"No, you stop it!" She got right in his face. "I didn't want to borrow money from you in the first place. I should have known there would be strings attached."

"I'm just trying to protect you." He captured her shoulders and ducked his head so he could look her in the eyes. "You do remember what happened the last time you let him into your life, right?"

"I can take care of myself, Mason." Kiera stared right back at him.

A muscle twitched in his jaw, but she didn't care. She would not allow her brother to steamroll his way over everything this time.

"Fine," Mason said. "It's not my call."

Trey walked up to them just then.

Mason shot him a murderous look. "You'd better not touch my sister."

Kiera threw her hands in the air. "What did we just discuss?"

"I'm sorry," he said. "I just…I don't like him around you."

"Mason, please, just let it go," she pleaded.

"Okay," he said, holding his hands up in mock surrender. He looked over at her, contriteness etched across his features. "I'm so damn sorry about throwing the money in your face, Kiera. Can we pretend that never happened?"

"How about I accept your apology and we move on?"

His self-deprecating grin went a long way to assuage Kiera's irritation. Staying upset with Mason was so hard to do, especially when she thought of everything he'd sacrificed for her.

"Thank you," he said. He gave her a quick peck on the cheek before starting for his car.

"Wait a minute," Kiera called. "You're here, don't you want to see the work that's been done on the truck?"

"No. Because if it looks good then I'll have to compliment that bastard."

Kiera clamped a hand around his wrist. "Stop being a big baby. And, please, behave."

Mason reluctantly allowed her to tug him to the truck. Even though the air was still fraught with tension, it lessened a bit as Trey explained the work he'd done so far. Her brother grudgingly acknowledged that the truck was shaping up nicely, and when Trey pointed out the change he'd made to the exhaust system, Mason even complimented him.

"I still can't stand your ass, but I have to

admit you're doing a good job here."

"I love you, too," Trey drawled.

Kiera rolled her eyes. She needed aspirin. Or tequila. Or both.

"Are you still coming over to mom's for dinner tomorrow?" Kiera asked Mason as she walked with him to his car.

"I'll be there," he answered. "I may be a little late, though. Matt Gauthier is trying to talk me into coming on as a consultant for a review of the state's tax credit law. We're meeting at Galatoire's at five for drinks."

"One of the most expensive restaurants in the French Quarter. Nice to see our tax dollars hard at work."

"Gotta love Louisiana politics," Mason said. He gave her another peck on the cheek. "I'll talk to you later." He gestured with his chin toward Trey. "You're still an asshole."

"Right back at you, bro," Trey called.

Kiera watched her brother leave then walked over to Trey's truck and plopped her butt against the lowered tailgate.

"I would have thought he'd have mellowed," Trey said, taking a seat next to her. "But now I remember that your brother has been that uptight since we were in kindergarten."

"Why do you two hate each other so much?"

"We didn't always," he said, grabbing a leaf from the tree branch that arched over his truck bed. "It's not that we were ever best friends or anything, but we used to get along ok."

"What changed?"

A mischievous grin lifted up the corner of his mouth. "I started banging his little sister." He shrugged. "Can't really blame the guy for hating me. If I were him, I'd be ready to murder me, too."

Kiera groaned and pushed her hands through her hair. "I know he means well, but I swear he drives me crazy sometimes. Mason thinks he can dictate my life. He always has."

"Looked to me like you did a pretty good job of letting him know that it's *your* life, not his."

"I did, didn't I?" she said, feeling a surge of pride that she'd stood up to her brother.

Trey nudged her with his elbow. "You really want to piss him off?" He leaned over and whispered in her ear, "Come over to my place and let me make you dinner."

She burst out laughing. "What am I going to do with you?" She quickly put a hand up. "Don't answer that."

Trey pitched his head back and barked out a laugh.

"Are you going to let me cook you dinner or not, Slim? I've got some mad skills." He nudged her again. "I know how to cook, too."

She shook her head, unsure if she was on the verge of laughing or crying. With the emotional seesaw both Trey and Mason had taken her on in the last twenty minutes, she could go either way.

She knew she should say no. If she said yes, Kiera knew she would be accepting so much more than an invitation to dinner.

But she could no longer lie to herself. She really wanted that more. She wanted that so much she ached with it.

"Okay," she finally said. "Show me your mad kitchen skills."

Trey layered several slices of cheddar on the thick sourdough before topping it with the second slice of bread.

"You want me to top off your glass?" he called to Kiera, who sat with her legs folded underneath her in the leather recliner in his living room.

"I'll finish what I have here and save the next glass for dinner," she said, taking a sip. "It's a lovely wine. Callie was telling Jada and I about this wine bar in New Orleans. I wonder if they carry this?"

"I'm not big on wines." Trey shrugged, shaving off several more slices of the aged cheddar. "This bottle was a gift from Lori. She brought it back from the trip she took to Italy a few years ago."

"Why didn't you save this for something special?" Kiera asked as he came into the living room.

He poised a sliver of cheese before her lips. "I did save it for something special."

Kiera regarded him with a wary look. "I thought this was just dinner, not Operation Seduction."

A grin edged up his mouth. "My intentions are completely virtuous."

"Uh huh," she murmured. She pointed the wineglass at his hand. "I can see you crossing your fingers." She leaned forward and allowed him to slip the cheese into her mouth. Her eyelids slid shut and a low, ridiculously sexy sound traveled from her throat.

"Good cheese," she said. "Nice and sharp."

Her satisfied moan tugged at a spot deep in his gut. It was just cheese, for goodness sake. How could watching the woman eat cheese turn him on so damn much?

"I told you I had mad skills," he said, returning to the stove.

Kiera laughed, springing up from the chair and following him into the kitchen.

"I'll admit I'm impressed. Most people go for the basic American; it takes a culinary genius to pair aged cheddar with sour dough."

"Are you done making fun of me?" he asked. "I may not have a degree like you, but I've managed not to starve over the years." He paused for a moment before he continued. "I'm proud of you for going back to culinary school once you finished at UNO, Slim. It's what *you* wanted to do, not what Mason wanted you to do. That bastard has always had too much control over your life."

"Don't talk bad about him," she said. "I know Mason was a jerk today, but he means well. He's just trying to do what's best for me."

"Do you really buy that, Kiera?"

"Trey, I owe Mason everything. He's been taking care of my mom and me since he was fourteen years old. It should have been the most enjoyable time of his life, but instead of going out and doing what other teens did, he spent it taking care of us."

Trey gnawed on the inside of his cheek while he listened to her defend her overbearing asshole of a brother.

"He didn't have to step up the way he did," Kiera continued. "But he did it anyway. Does he take the whole big brother thing overboard sometimes…?"

"*Some*times?"

"Okay, a lot of the time," she said. "But it has always been to protect me. He really isn't a bad guy, Trey. I know you two don't see eye to eye on a lot of things, but you've been gone a long time, you don't know Mason now."

"I know what I saw this afternoon."

"That was…"

"That was him trying to control you."

"That was him just being him. Believe me,

today wasn't the first time I've had to put him in his place. But Mason doesn't see himself as being controlling; he thinks he's helping. In his mind, he still has to live up to that promise he made my dad, that he would take care of me and mom."

"You're a grown woman, Kiera. You don't need your big brother taking care of you anymore." Trey ran a finger softly down her cheek. She was so close. Just another couple of inches and he could have another taste of that mouth. It had been all he could think about since the last time he'd tasted it.

"The sandwiches," Kiera said, pulling back slightly.

He suffered through the swift pang of regret that dashed through him and returned his attention to the stove. Ten minutes later, they were seated at the one-of-a-kind table he'd hewn out of old doors he'd found in a scrapyard in East Texas. He refilled Kiera's wineglass, then took a sip of the beer he'd opted for.

"I'm being totally serious when I say that this sandwich is amazing," she said before popping a chunk of the buttery crust into her mouth.

"I wanted to impress you, for obvious reasons. Have I done a good job?"

Shaking her head, she said, "You're still such a flirt."

"You used to like it when I flirted with you."

"I used to live for it," she admitted. She swirled her spoon around the bowl of tomato soup he'd picked up at the supermarket deli, then she looked up at him and said, "You were so bad for me in so many ways, Trey. But I loved it. Speeding down Highway 421 in your GTO, skinny-dipping in Ponderosa Pond, finishing off an entire bottle of Boone's Farm while we watched horror movies at your house. If my mother knew I was drinking liquor at eighteen..."

He waved that off. "Boone's Farm isn't real liquor."

She laughed. "I guess what they say is true, the good girls always go for the bad boys."

He braced his elbow on either side of his plate and rested his lips on his folded hands. He hated what he was about to ask, but it had been on his mind almost as much as that kiss they'd shared.

"So, has that been the case over the years, Slim? You've gone for the bad boys?"

She tilted her head to the side and regarded him thoughtfully. "Actually, no," she said. "Just the opposite, in fact. The guys I've dated in the past have been completely different from you."

Now that he'd asked, Trey wished he could take back the question. Even though he was the one who'd walked away, the thought of Kiera with someone else slayed him. After all the time that had passed, he still had a hard time thinking of her as anything but his.

Despite the sudden nausea churning in his gut, Trey continued with the questions he didn't really want answers to. He cleared his throat, then asked, "Were any of them serious?"

She ran her finger along the rim of her wineglass. "It depends on what you define as serious."

"I'm assuming you would have told me if you'd ever been married, but was there anyone who ever came close?"

She brought her wineglass to her lips and took a long, deliberate sip. After several torturous moments, she finally answered with a simple, straightforward, "No."

"No?" Trey asked, wanting to make sure he'd heard her correctly.

"I've never come close," she said. "I've had a couple of serious boyfriends, but not a single one has made me feel as if I wanted to spend the rest of my life with them."

He should have been euphoric over her admission, but instead, Trey felt…sad. He could see in her eyes just how much she wanted that special kind of happiness. And if anyone deserved to be happy, it was Kiera.

"There's still time."

"That's what I tell myself," she said, a bittersweet smile tilting her lips. "It's especially hard, seeing both Jada and Callie find love again, but I have to believe my Prince Charming is out there somewhere, right?"

Trey fiddled with the edge of his napkin before saying in a low voice, "Maybe he's even closer than you think."

The air around them hummed with expectancy as she stared at him across the table. Without giving himself time to question what he was doing, Trey pushed away from the table and walked over to Kiera. He leaned forward and threaded his fingers through the hair at her nape. Gently, he tugged her head closer.

She put up zero resistance, slanting her head to the side and running her hands over his shoulders. Her lips quickly parted and she sucked his tongue inside the moist warmth of her mouth. It was slightly sweet, slightly tart with the essence of the wine she'd enjoyed with dinner.

Back and forth he moved over her mouth, plunging and retreating, savoring her flavor. Her taste was potent; the feelings she stirred inside him drugging his senses. His fingertips tingled as he caressed behind her ear, her hair flittering softly over his skin. He stroked his tongue deep inside her mouth, gliding it along her teeth before plunging even further. He mimicked with his mouth what he wanted to do to her with his body, what he was *dying* to do to her.

"Damn, Slim," Trey whispered against her lips. "Tell me now if you want to stop, because I won't unless you say something."

She shook her head. "I don't want to stop."

No sweeter words had ever been spoken.

His entire body damn near trembling in anticipation, Trey lifted her from the seat at the table and carried her to the sofa. He sat down and placed her on top of him so that she straddled his hips. He could feel the heat radiating from her. It sparked an equal reaction within him. Anticipation pumped through his veins like lava, his heart turning over in his chest as his gaze traveled up her body.

He wanted her so much every fiber in his body hummed with desire.

He moved her until her hot center was aligned perfectly with his straining erection, and held her in place while he pumped his hips upward. He was hard as hell. The need to strip them both of their clothes and fill Kiera with his body was so strong, so incredibly overpowering, that he couldn't think of anything else.

Trey tunneled his fingers underneath the stretchy fabric of her T-shirt, gripping her back. He loved the softness of her skin, the smoothness of it against the roughness of his fingertips. But taking the time to truly relish in the suppleness of her delicate skin would have to wait. Right now, his body was screaming to experience the magic that only Kiera could create.

Trey plunged his hands into her waistband

and gripped her ass.

"Oh, God, Trey," Kiera breathed. Her head fell back, exposing her neck to his lips.

As she held onto his shoulders, Trey explored the column of her neck, pulling the skin between his teeth, licking and biting and devouring her.

He needed her naked, in his bed, her legs wrapped around his hips, her hot, wet sex clutching his cock.

Trey scooped one arm under her bottom and fitted the other hand on her back. He picked her up and carried her to his bed.

Stripping his shirt over his head, he threw it behind him and then did the same with his pants. His stomach clutched with need as he watched Kiera roll her pants down her legs and fling them off her foot. She peeled her shirt off and sent it the way of her pants. Then she scooted to the center of his bed in only her white cotton undies and bra. For some reason, the innocent underwear made her even sexier than if she wore sheer and lace.

"God, you're beautiful, Slim. So damn beautiful."

He crawled onto the bed and covered her body with his, dipping his head down and going straight for her breasts. He sucked her through the cotton bra, soaking the fabric until her dusky brown nipples showed through.

It was hard as hell not to strip off the rest of

their clothes and fill her body with his, but this was fourteen years in the making, and he wasn't rushing it for anything. Instead, Trey took his time, revisiting every inch of her. He pressed a kiss to her flat stomach, his pulse throbbing with desire as he trailed his tongue from her bellybutton to the shallow valley between her breasts. Pleasure coursed through his veins with every lick of her deliciously feminine skin.

"I love how you taste," Trey murmured against the underside of her breast.

He hooked his fingers in both sides of her underwear and rolled them down her hips, his lips following her panties as he peppered her smooth thighs and legs with kisses. He tossed her panties aside and made the journey back up her body.

He spotted the tiny tattoo on her hip and his chest nearly burst with the emotion that suddenly filled it.

"The rose," Trey let out with a husky breath, staring at the miniature version of the tattoo he had on his chest. Memories of the day they'd gotten them rushed through him. Trey pressed a kiss to the symbol of the love they'd shared, his mark on her.

He trailed his lips along her skin, coming to the spot that his entire being was hungry for. Rubbing delicate circles along her inner thighs with his thumbs, Trey then used them to open her legs wide. His eyes briefly slid shut as he pulled in a deep breath.

God, he wanted her. He'd dreamed of her. Wished for her. But never thought he'd have her again.

But he did.

And he was going to eat up every single bit of her.

Dipping his head between her legs, he spread her sex open with his fingers and ran his tongue slowly up and down her center. Pleasure exploded in his brain as her familiar flavor hit his tongue.

The sexy little noise that escaped Kiera's throat only fueled his desire to please her more. He hooked his arms underneath her thighs and brought them over his shoulders, then he tilted her pelvis so that she was at an even better angle.

Trey lost all concept of time as he made up for all the years that had passed since he'd last had a taste of her, experiencing a new high with every low murmur that escaped her lips. He continued to bathe her with his tongue, licking and sucking her into his mouth, until she came twice.

Her body was still trembling from her second orgasm when he levered himself up, rolled a condom over his erection and slid slowly and deeply inside of her.

This is what he remembered. Ecstasy. Pure, sweet ecstasy.

Trey's head pitched back. "God, Kiera," he released between clinched teeth.

His eyes squeezed shut; his arms strained to the point of trembling. Yet he managed to hold himself still as he soaked in the feeling of being surrounded by Kiera again. Every thought, every part of his being concentrated on the heat, the snug feel of her, the absolute perfect fit; it was everything he remembered.

She wrapped her legs around him, crossing her ankles at the small of his back.

"Trey…please."

Her desperately whispered plea called to his most primitive side, but Trey held himself back. He wanted this to last; was desperate to please her.

With slow, deliberate thrusts, he began to move his hips against her, rocking back and forth, in and out, slow and long and deep.

Trey managed to keep up the unhurried pace until Kiera lifted up from the bed and started placing open-mouth kisses along the flower vine tattoo that wound it's way across his chest. She kissed the blood red rose tattooed over his heart, the one that mirrored hers.

Trey dipped his head and glided his tongue along her neck and up to her jaw. "It still belongs to you," he said.

Trey felt her shudder at his words and it was more than his body could withstand. He anchored his hands on her waist and drove into her with deep, rapid thrusts, circling his hips before lunging as far as he could go.

Their twin cries rang out in the small confines of the Bluebird. Trey's head fell forward and their heavy breaths mingled together.

Several minutes passed before he managed to say, "God, that was good."

"Better than I remembered," Kiera breathed.

He looked down at her and grinned. "I don't know about that, Slim. We were always good together."

"I know," she said. She released a heavy sigh. "Sometimes I still can't believe it was only one summer."

The reminder of the brevity of their time together sent a piercing ache slicing straight through him. His chest constricting with a flood of emotion, Trey said, "Maybe this time it won't end."

Kiera looked up at him, her eyes slowly widening in dismay. "Oh, my God," she said. "Oh, my God. What did I just do?"

"Kiera—"

Dread pooled in his stomach as he watched realization dawn in her eyes.

"No," she said. "I told myself I would not let this happen." She pushed at his chest at the same time she slid from underneath him and scooted off the bed. "I need to leave."

She spun around in a hasty circle, lifting the articles of clothing that lay strewn across the floor. Trey reached for her, narrowly missing her arm as she scuttled out of the bedroom and past the kitchen.

"Kiera, would you wait a minute?"

"No," she said. "I told myself when I hired you that I would *not* let this happen." She nearly tripped as she tried to pull her jeans on and walk at the same time. She pulled her shirt over her head and grabbed her purse from where she'd tossed it on the sofa when she'd first arrived.

"Dammit, Slim. Don't do this."

She put a hand up. "This is…this was stupid. *So* stupid. I know better than to let you in like this. I need to…I need to go."

He reached for her again, but she jerked away from him and was out of the bus.

Trey braced his hands on the wall and pulled in several deep breaths.

"Dammit," he whispered again. So much for his skills of seduction.

Kiera stood in the hallway of her condo building, staring at the elevator doors. She caught herself biting her fingernail and jerked her hand from her mouth.

She'd spotted Callie and Jada's cars as they both pulled into the parking lot within a minute of each other, so she knew they would be up here any second. The elevator dinged and the doors opened. She rushed over and was waiting when they both walked off the elevator.

"Come on, come on, come on," Kiera said, grabbing each by the wrist and dragging them toward her condo.

"Hey, you want to ease up? I'm not a rag doll," Jada said, trying to jerk her arm free.

"Kiera, what's going on?" Callie asked. "What's with the urgent meeting? Are you okay?"

She ushered them into the condo, closed the door, and fell back against it.

"No," she finally answered. "I am definitely *not* okay."

Callie and Jada both rushed to her side. "What's wrong? What happened?"

Kiera thumped her head back against the door and covered her face with her hands. "I slept with Trey Watson."

"What!" Callie and Jada shrieked in unison.

Kiera slumped down to the floor, brought her knees up and rested her forehead on them.

"Oh, my God!" Callie said. "Where did you even see him, Kiera?"

"Was he still good?" Jada asked.

Callie slapped her on the arm, and then stooped down until she was eye-level with Kiera. "Honey, how in the world did you end up sleeping with Trey?"

"He's renovating my food truck," she said.

"Holy crap!" Jada yelped. "*Trey* is the

person you hired to work on the truck? Mason is going to lose his shit over this."

"He already did. He came over to the truck today while Trey was working on it. I had to stop them from punching each other at least three times."

"We need wine," Callie said. "Lots and lots of wine."

"I've got white in the fridge." Kiera allowed Jada to pull her up from the floor. She trudged over to the L-shaped sofa that was a gift from her mother when she moved into this condo two years ago.

"Brownies?" Callie asked as she came into the living room and set the wine and glasses on the coffee table.

Kiera shook her head.

"No brownies?" Jada asked. "You're a caterer. Caterers should always have brownies."

"Do you have *anything* sweet?" Callie asked.

"I've been so busy at the kitchen that I haven't had a chance to cook much here. I think I have a can of chocolate frosting in the pantry," she offered.

"Works for me," Jada said.

Moments later, Callie perched herself on the chaise, cradling the can of frosting and three spoons.

"Okay, spill it," she said.

They each scooped up a spoonful of frosting and Kiera began explaining how Mychal had hooked her up with Trey.

"I knew he had recommended someone to work on the truck, but you never said it was Trey Watson," Jada said.

"I know." She kneaded her temples. "I didn't say anything because I had no intention of contacting him, but then I saw some of the other work he'd done and knew he was the person for the job. He's really good at what he does." Callie and Jada both gave her identical, probing looks. "He's good at renovating trucks," Kiera clarified. "And, yeah, at other stuff, too."

"I knew it," Jada said. "I used to be so jealous when you would talk about how good he was in bed."

"I was an eighteen year old virgin, Jada. I didn't know what constituted good or bad in bed."

Her friend huffed out a cynical breath. "I knew Eric wasn't good," she said, speaking of her ex-husband.

Kiera brought her legs up on the sofa and dropped her head to her knees. "God, how could I be so stupid?"

Jada waved that off as she reached for more wine. "Honey, please. Every girl in this town was stupid for Trey Watson at one time or another."

"Does he still have that sexy little dip in his bottom lip?" Callie asked.

"And that butt!" Jada said, high-fiving

Callie. "Trey had the finest ass in all of Maplesville High."

"Would you two stop! You're supposed to be helping me figure out just what I'm going to do, not commenting on the man's ass. Which, by the way, is as fine as ever."

Kiera groaned and dropped her head to her knees again.

How on earth could she let this happen? She knew better than to sleep with him. Once she gave him her body, her heart wouldn't be far off. And of all the stupid things she could ever do, giving her heart to Trey again would be the stupidest.

Because he would break it again when he left.

And he *would* leave. As soon as he was done with the renovation, he would pack up that cute little Bluebird bus and return to his old life, leaving her once again with a shattered heart.

Kiera rested her chin on her knees. "What am I going to do?"

"What are your choices?" Callie asked.

"Well, the first choice is to not let my panties drop the next time I'm around him."

"You sure that would be a bad thing?" Jada asked. "What?" she asked, looking back and forth between Kiera and Callie. "You can't tell me Garrett was a rock star between the sheets. At least with Trey you're getting a known quantity."

Kiera groaned again. "You're no help at all."

"Sorry," she said, draining her wineglass.

"Are you sure there's no one else who can work on the truck?" Callie asked.

"I don't have time to find anyone else, and honestly, I don't want to. Not only is he doing a fabulous job, but he's doing it for an amazingly low price."

"Maybe that's because he expects to be paid in some other way," Callie suggested with a pointed look.

"If I were you, I'd take that deal," Jada said. "Just watch out for your heart. You know what Trey did to it the last time."

They all knew what Trey had done to her heart, and she was not going to allow herself to go through that again. She was older now. Wiser. She would be a fool to purposely expose herself like that again.

"Okay," Kiera said, stiffening her spine. "It's simple. I resist him."

"*Is* it that simple?" Callie asked with a skeptical frown.

"It has to be. The shrimp festival is only a couple of weeks away. It's not as if I can have him stop work on the truck just because I want to get naked for him whenever I see him."

Jada pointed a frosting-laden spoon at her. "That gets my vote. Think of how much fun you and Trey can have naked. And if you bring some of the toys you bought at my last Naughty

Nights party, you two can have a *lot* of fun."

"Don't listen to her," Callie said, then she looked over at Jada. "But you just reminded me that I need some of that gel stuff that turns hot then cold."

"Isn't that stuff amazing?" Jada asked. "Stefan loves it!"

"Mason, too. Especially when I rub it—"

Kiera held up a hand. "Okay, first, eww," she said to Jada. "How many times do we have to have the 'No Sex Talk When You're Sleeping With My Brother' discussion?"

"That's not fair." Jada pouted. "You two get to talk about your sex lives."

"Deal with it," Kiera said. "There will never be a time when I'm okay with hearing about Mason in the bedroom. And we're supposed to be discussing how I should *not* be having sex with Trey."

"Fine," Jada mumbled, crossing her arms and sitting back in her chair.

Callie reached over and put a hand on Kiera's thigh. "Look, honey. No matter what happens, the best advice I can give you is to just be careful. We all know how in love you were with Trey at one time. It would be very easy to get sucked into that again."

"Callie's right," Jada said. "The most important thing is that you protect your heart. Neither of us wants to see you get hurt."

And therein lay her problem. She was pretty

sure her stupid heart was already well on its way to loving him again.

Chapter Six

"Dad? *Dad*?" RJ whispered from several feet away. "Look at that one?"

Trey glanced in the direction his son pointed and spotted a pale green grasshopper that matched the color of the blade of grass it balanced upon. He held a finger to his lips and stealthily made his way to the grasshopper, crossing over a thick, moss-covered fallen tree trunk. He hoped like hell the thing didn't jump on him.

Holding the specimen jar in one hand and the lid in the other, he came at the grasshopper from the rear and was able to snatch him up.

"Got him," Trey said.

"Yes!" RJ did a fist pump and came running. "That's a big one!" He took the jar from Trey. "I'm going to put him at the center of my ecosystem. Unless we find one bigger," he tacked on.

Trey suppressed a shudder.

He was man enough to admit that when it came to insects he wasn't the biggest fan, which is why it seemed like the most hilarious cosmic joke that of the list of projects Roland Jr. had to choose from for his science class—one that included building a catapult out of rubber bands and Ping-Pong balls, which would have been cool as *hell*—his son had chosen to put together an ecosystem with insects indigenous to southern Louisiana.

Trey's first impulse had been to talk him out of the insect project, but that was something his own father, who used to tell Trey he was wasting his time fixing cars, would have done.

He would not do that to *his* son. Hell no.

Did he get a slight thrill at the thought of spending an entire afternoon working on the '69 Camaro with RJ at his side? Of course, he did. But that wasn't his son's deal. If he wasn't playing a computer game, RJ had his face in a book. Trey wasn't sure the boy even knew what a socket wrench looked like.

So what if RJ preferred real bugs to Volkswagen Bugs? As he observed him scouring the dank grounds, Trey realized it didn't matter one damn bit if RJ never looked underneath the hood of a car. What mattered was that Trey was here for both RJ and Rachel.

Last night, he'd reached a decision that would allow that to be more than just an aspiration for some time in the future. He'd decided to make being here for his kids a part of his permanent reality.

They spent the next two hours in search of a list of insects RJ had received from his science teacher. Trey was still blown away that the kids had such an involved homework assignment so early into the school year. Eighth-grade was a lot more intense than when he was in school.

By the time Angie called to say that she and Rachel were on their way back from their day of pampering—a reward Rach had earned for having finished her science project already—he and RJ had collected all but two of the insects listed.

Trey pulled into the parking lot of the filling station on Highway 190 where he'd met Angie earlier to pick up RJ.

"How was the insect hunting?" his ex-wife asked as he walked RJ to her Lexus SUV. A smirk tilted up the corner of her mouth. "Enjoy yourself?"

Trey grinned. "We were married long enough for you to know just how enjoyable I found it."

Angie's head flew back with her laugh. "Think of all the great father/son bonding time."

"That's what it's all about," he said, giving RJ two solid pats on the back. He leaned in the open back window and gave Rachel a kiss.

"We're still going out for bowling and pizza before you go back to Houston, right?" Rachel asked.

Trey hesitated for a second, debating whether he should share the decision he'd come to with the kids just yet. He decided to hold off until his plans were more concrete.

He nodded. "Pizza and bowling it is. And don't forget I'm taking you guys to the Louisiana Shrimp Festival. I heard they're supposed to have some kind of carnival ride that spins you around until you throw up."

That earned excited whoops from the kids and an eye-roll from Angie.

Laughing, Trey waved goodbye, watching as she pulled back onto the highway. It had taken him a while to realize it, but he was lucky as hell to have someone as understanding as Angie as a partner in raising his children. Their marriage hadn't been ideal, and he had not done a damn thing to make it better. Angie had, though. At least she'd tried. Even though she knew he had been in love with someone else, she'd tried to make it work for those first few years.

He didn't deserve all the chances she'd given him, the forgiveness she'd bestowed. He gratefully accepted it, and he did everything he could to make things easier for her.

Which is why, even though they had joint custody, Trey hadn't put up a fuss when she'd told him about Donald's job transferring them to Louisiana. He'd signed the required paperwork granting her permission to move the kids out of state and had set up a schedule to visit at least once a month, or whenever his work schedule allowed.

But that once a month deal wasn't going to

cut it. He needed to be here for his kids all the time. And he would.

He was moving back to Maplesville. Permanently.

It occurred to him last night, just after he'd made next month's payment on the land he leased to park the Bluebird, that there was no reason for him to return to Houston. Maplesville could be his home base and he could simply fly out to wherever his work took him. Moving back to Maplesville meant he could have a true presence in his kids' lives, not this once-a-month shit.

He wouldn't have to worry about finding renovation jobs anytime soon, either. He'd spent some time lurking on the online food truck forums these past couple of weeks, and it was obvious that the New Orleans area was packed with eager entrepreneurs champing at the bit to try their luck at running a mobile kitchen. He'd even shared a couple of private messages with a few of them. Finding work would be no problem at all.

Of the many advantages that came with the decision to remain in Maplesville, there was one that made the blood in his veins boil over with desire.

Kiera.

A sharp ache stabbed his chest just at the thought of her.

In the five days since she'd run from his

home, all of their communication had been via text message, and strictly about the food truck. He had a collection of her short, curt, dispassionate responses stored in his phone. Trey brought up their need to talk about what happened back at the Bluebird after dinner on Monday night, but those texts went unanswered.

Instead of pushing her further, he'd focused all his energy on the renovations, deciding that maybe it was for the best that he and Kiera go back to the strictly professional relationship she'd first insisted on.

But that was bullshit.

He wasn't giving up this easily. He'd let her go once; he wasn't making that mistake again.

Trey got in his truck and headed back to Maplesville. He drove past the exit that would take him to the Bluebird and continued traveling east, toward the condo building where Kiera had mentioned she lived.

He entered the building and was staggered by the multitier chandelier and marble lobby. Luxury on this scale didn't fit in a small town like Maplesville.

The reality of just how different he and Kiera still were hit Trey square in the chest. It didn't matter that he could have probably purchased two of the condos in this building with the money he had in the bank; the fact that he was living in a school bus while she lived in the ritziest place in town struck at the very core of the barrier that had always stood between them.

No matter what he had accomplished in his life, he would never truly be good enough for a girl like Kiera Coleman.

But he was determined to make her his anyway.

Because despite the difference in their backgrounds, despite all the people who said the two of them didn't fit, he loved her, and Trey knew she loved him, too.

He had hoped to find a board of some sort with the occupants and their condo numbers, but there was none, so he took out his phone and hoped for the best.

I'm downstairs, he texted Kiera. *Please let me up.*

A full minute passed before his phone dinged with a text with her floor number and instructions to come up.

Trey's heart started to pound with anticipation as he boarded the elevator for the seventh floor. When he stepped from the car, Kiera was waiting for him outside her door. His eyes never left hers as he made his way down the hallway.

"Hey," she greeted.

One simple word, but it was enough to make his bones wilt in relief. She was talking to him again.

She took a step back and opened the door wider. "Come in."

It had only been five days since he'd last seen her, yet it seemed like a lifetime ago. How had he managed to stay away for fourteen years?

"Thanks for letting me come up," Trey said, moving out of the way so she could close the door behind him. "I was afraid you would demand all contact remain text only."

A wry, self-deprecating grin etched across her lips. "I think I reached my childish behavior quota when I hightailed it out of your bus earlier this week." She looked up at him. "I apologize for that, and for ignoring your attempts to talk about it."

The sincere regret in her eyes gave Trey hope. If she were sorry for leaving, maybe she would be willing to stick around the next time.

And the next time. And the next time.

"So, can we talk about it now?" Trey asked.

She pulled in a breath so deep that her chest expanded with it. "Yes," she said, "but I think I'm going to need a drink first."

She headed through a square archway, leaving him alone in the tastefully decorated living room. Trey turned around in a slow circle, taking in her home. It was exactly the kind of place he'd expect her to live. Not too cluttered, but not particularly sparse, either.

He walked over to a six-tier shelf in the corner and studied the framed photographs. There was her high school graduation picture, and one he assumed was from her college graduation. There were several of her standing outside the Catering by Kiera building during different phases of its construction, and then the one with her, Mason and their parents. Kiera must have been about eight or nine years old at the time. Trey remembered it being on her dresser back when they were dating.

His stomach tightened when he spotted a shiny black rock on the second shelf.

He picked up the onyx pebble and rubbed it between his fingers. He turned at the sound of approaching footsteps and held the rock up to Kiera.

"You've kept this all this time?"

She nodded as she handed him a bottle of water. With a delicate shrug, she said, "How could I bring myself to throw it away?"

"I remember that day," he said, rolling the cool stone around in his palm. The two of them had been out at Ponderosa Pond, sitting on the tailgate of his dad's old truck. It was the first time he'd told her he loved her.

"We need to talk about the other night," Trey said.

"I know," she said. "But not yet."

"Kiera—"

She put up both hands. "Okay, fine. Eventually, yes, we'll need to talk about the other night and about how I've acted like an immature ass by avoiding you for the past five days. I really am sorry about that, Trey. But could we not talk about that right this second? If we do, it will only kill my buzz."

He took note of the excited gleam sparkling in her eyes. "What's got you buzzed?"

She held her phone up to him. "My recipe was chosen as a finalist! The email came while I was in the kitchen!"

"Holy shit! Congratulations, Slim!" Trey said, picking her up and spinning her around. He set her down, but didn't let go of her waist. It felt so damn good to hold her again. "We've got to do something to celebrate."

Her brows drew together as a hint of distrust entered her eyes. "Exactly what do you mean when you say '*some*thing.'"

His grin grew so wide it made his cheeks hurt. "That's not what I was thinking," Trey said. "I've got something else in mind."

Kiera slurped the last of the creamy root beer float, and frowned at the bottom of her cup. She eyed Trey's, which was still half full and sitting next to his hip, while his upper body lay stretched out on a mechanic's creeper underneath a red '69 Camaro that was hitched up with a hydraulic jack.

She'd had to laugh when, after buying celebratory floats from Hannah's Ice Cream

Parlor, he'd continued going east to Gauthier and, twenty minutes later had pulled into Decker Anderson's auto service garage. What girl wouldn't choose a repair shop that hadn't been used in years as a place to celebrate?

But Kiera wasn't complaining. This place held some of the very best memories from her carefree teenage years.

Perched on a table in the center of the shop, Kiera crossed her feet at the ankles and swung her legs back and forth. "Are you going to finish your float?" she asked.

"Yes!" Trey called. "Don't touch my cup."

"Not fair. I'm the one who's celebrating."

He rolled the mechanic's creeper from underneath the car and looked up at her.

"You're also the one who insisted on getting the smallest size because you're watching your waistline." He snorted. "As if you're not skinny enough."

"Hey! It's not my fault I have an accelerated metabolism."

"I'm not complaining," he said. "I like you slim, Slim."

"What if I'd packed on an extra thirty pounds over the years, huh? What would you have to say about that?"

Trey regarded her for several moments. Finally, in a decidedly husky voice, he said, "I would tell you those pounds are perfection on you."

A delicious warmth cascaded through her, both at the words he'd spoken and the enticing way he'd said them.

"You're just saying that to make up for not sharing your root beer float," Kiera said in an effort to stave off the heat that was steadily building in the air around them.

Trey pushed himself up from the cradle of the creeper. "I'm saying that because it is the absolute truth. No other reason." He handed her his cup. "Drink up. You deserve it." He hoisted himself up on the table. "Although, come to think of it, I'm celebrating a bit, too."

Kiera glanced over at him with a raised brow.

"I had a really good day out with RJ today," he explained. "We worked on his school project, and talked about him possibly trying out for band next year." He let out a soft chuckle. "We even talked about this girl in his class that he sort of likes."

"Uh oh. Don't tell me daddy gave him pointers about women."

The smile that traced across his lips was just short of devastating. Goodness, but he was gorgeous.

"I just told him to be himself. RJ is a pretty cool kid, he doesn't need to pretend to be anything he's not," Trey said. "He's thinking of asking her to their fall dance." He ran his hand down his face and let out a sigh. "This stage came way too quickly. I'm not sure if I'm ready to be the father of a kid who dates. I sure as hell won't be ready to have this conversation with Rachel."

"This is so adorable." She laughed. "And a bit hilarious."

"What?"

"The thought of you, of all people, being an overprotective dad."

"Shit. You know what, I'm starting to understand where Mason was coming from. If Rachel ever brought home a guy like me, I don't know what I'd do."

"You weren't so bad." He sent her a wry look. "Okay, you were bad enough, but you've changed." Kiera nudged him with her elbow. "It looks good on you, you know? Being a dad, especially one who's so concerned."

He shrugged. "They make me want to be better." He glanced over at the root beer float in her hand. "Damn, that looks good. I knew I should have kept it."

Laughing, Kiera handed him the drink.

He held it up and peered at the nearly empty cup.

"Thanks a lot." His dry tone only made her laugh harder. Trey took one sip and tossed the plastic cup into a rusty oil drum. He toed the engine hoist, moving its steel leg back and forth along the roller. "Being here really brings you back, doesn't it?"

"Oh, yeah. I became pretty familiar with this old place that summer. It's as muggy as ever, too," she said, peeling off the shirt she wore unbuttoned over a tank top.

"That's because Decker didn't believe in conventional things like air conditioning. The only reason there's still electricity is because it's tied to the house. Corey doesn't have the heart to close it up yet." His eyes roamed around the space. "The place is still in pretty good shape. It wouldn't take much to get it up and running again."

It was on the tip of her tongue to ask him if he would give any thought to taking over the garage, but Kiera didn't want to kill the relaxed mood between them, and she knew if Trey didn't say the answer she wanted to hear, *her* mood would be shot to hell.

He was leaving. She'd come to terms with that over these past five days. He would be done with her truck in less than two weeks, and then he would be gone.

She thought the safest course to guard against falling for him again would be to stay away, but she'd already fallen. Staying away from him this week had done nothing but cost her five extra days she could have spent with the man who had always owned her heart. Kiera decided that she would enjoy having him back in her life while she still had him, and deal with whatever heartbreak that followed once he was gone.

She'd done it before; she could do it again.

Kiera lifted her shoulders up to her ears and pulled in a deep breath. The air was redolent with fragrant memories from her past. "I won't lie, Trey, I used to love coming here with you."

He opened his mouth, and then closed it. Shaking his head, he said, "That was way too easy, Slim. I'm not even going to touch it."

Kiera thought for a moment then slapped his arm. "Stop making everything about sex. It wasn't all about sex."

Trey lolled his head to the side and stared at her, a knowing, amused expression lighting his eyes.

"Okay, fine," she conceded. "When I followed you out here to Decker's, nine times out of ten it was about sex."

"Ten times out of ten, Slim. If the old cars in the lot behind this garage could talk..."

Her cheeks heated with the memories of that summer. How many times had they snuck away while he was working here at Decker's? Way too many to count. It was the place where she gave him her virginity. And the place where she'd continued to give herself to him over and over and over again, whenever they could steal away the time.

"It's a good thing those cars can't talk," Kiera mused. "I think Mason would kill you if he ever discovered half the things we used to do here."

"God knows he spent enough time looking for a reason to kill me. He's probably hiring a hit man as we speak."

Kiera's shoulders slumped with her sigh. "I swear, my life would be so much less complicated if the two of you could just get along."

"Not gonna happen."

"Why not?" She asked with an earnest plea. "Would it be so hard for two grown men to even *pretend* to like each other?"

"Kiera, the hate between your brother and me is not an act," Trey said. He kicked at the hoist with enough force to send it sailing across the garage floor. "Mason spent that entire summer doing everything he could to show me that I wasn't good enough for you."

"It wasn't just about you. He would have been distrustful of anyone I dated."

He gave her that sardonic look again, but this time there was no humor behind it. "Somehow I have a hard time believing he would have objected to you dating Chase Thomas or Desmond Hamilton or one of those other guys who grew up in a big house over on Dogwood Drive."

"Yes, he would have," Kiera insisted.

Trey's answer was a grunt.

"Look, I know Mason can be a bit irrational when it comes to you, but he has always had my best interest at heart, Trey."

"Your brother wants to control you. He always has. Shit, that's the reason you came sniffing after me in the first place. Or don't you remember?"

"Of course I remember, and yes, I know that Mason has always been overprotective—"

"Controlling."

"Concerned," she corrected.

"Yeah, well, you need to stop allowing your brother to be so *concerned* about everything that goes on in your life. As far as I can tell, he still thinks he has the right to have an opinion about everything you do."

"Look, I'm not giving Mason's tactics a pass, but the motives behind them have always been pure. And it looks as if he was right to warn me against you, doesn't it? Just look at how things turned out."

Several weighty moments ticked by before Trey's frustrated voice broke through the silence. "You still think that was my fault, don't you? That's the reason you left the other night after we made love, because you still blame me for us breaking up."

"Of course I blame you," Kiera said. She put her hands up. "Leaving you the way I did the other night was childish. I'll own up to that. It was cowardly and immature, but that's part of the problem, Trey. When I'm around you I feel like that silly little love struck girl who let you in and had her heart broken."

Looking straight ahead at the empty tire racks lining the wall, he said quietly, "You weren't the only one whose heart was broken back then."

Kiera sucked in a shocked breath. "Are you saying *I* broke *your* heart? *You're* the one who left! You left with zero explanation, just some bullshit about how this wasn't going to work. The next thing I hear, you're in Texas."

"And you never tried to find out why I left," he said.

"Why should I have? I would have looked like a fool running after you after the way you left me."

"Why don't you ask me now, Kiera?" he said, his hushed voice goading her. "Ask me why I left."

She scooted off the table and walked over to the shelves littered with tarnished cans and broken tools. She crossed her arms over her chest and said, "It was a long time ago. It doesn't matter."

"Yes, it does."

"Maybe to you, but I don't care enough to want to know."

"Yes, you do," Trey said. He walked up alongside her and assumed the pose she held. Staring at the rusty remnants of the place that had been such a meaningful part of their past, he quietly said, "You can't tell me that it hasn't bugged you all these years. You want to know why a lowlife like Trey Watson, who should have thanked his lucky stars that a girl like Kiera Coleman would even give him the time of day, had the audacity to just walk away."

She swallowed past a lump that had formed in her throat. "You know I never thought of you that way."

"Didn't you?"

She turned to him and frowned. "Why would you ask me something like that? I never treated you as if you were beneath me, not even once. And I think it's a shitty thing for you to insinuate that I did."

His nonchalant shrug only infuriated her more.

He reached forward and picked up a couple of corroded lug nuts from among the derelict items strewn across the shelf. He rolled them around in his palm before tossing them back on the shelf. Stuffing his hands in his front pockets, he pivoted on his heel and headed back toward the center of the garage.

After several awkward moments passed, he finally spoke. "Do you remember the weekend you moved into your college dorm?" He turned, looking at her over his shoulder. "Your mom was supposed to help you move, but you convinced her you could do it on your own? Then I sneaked and helped you instead."

She nodded, but didn't say anything.

"When Mason found out I was the one taking you to school, he went ballistic."

"He tended to do that often when it came to anything concerning me and you," Kiera said.

"True." He paused. "Did you know he came to see me that same weekend?"

"No, he didn't. He was studying for the LSAT. That's why he couldn't drive in from Baton Rouge to help me move."

"Yeah, well, he found some time away from his studying once he discovered I was the one bringing you to school."

Kiera dropped her face into her palms. "Please don't tell me you two had a fight I never knew about?"

"No." Trey shook his head. "In fact, the smug bastard was gloating. He told me that he'd been waiting for the day you left for school, because it didn't matter that you were only going to be an hour away, once you got on that campus and had your first taste of college life, you would forget about me."

"You know that wasn't true, Trey. We talked about it before I left for school. Nothing was supposed to change. We'd already made plans—"

"Yeah, I remember," he said, cutting her off. "We'd made plans to see each other every weekend. I'd drive out to New Orleans, or you'd come home to Maplesville. The couple no one thought should be together would show everybody just how much they were meant for each other."

His mocking tone made Kiera flinch. "I was serious when I made those plans with you," she managed to get out past the hurt squeezing her throat. "Apparently, it was all a joke to you."

He twisted around to face her. "You think *I'm* the one who made a joke out of our relationship?" He laughed, but there was no humor in it. After another pause, he continued. "I received several other visits from Mason during those first couple of months after you left for school. He hated—absolutely *hated*—the fact that we were still together. He tried to order me to leave you alone, as if that had ever worked before. Then he tried to pay me off."

Kiera's eyes slid shut. "God, Mason," she whispered.

"But, you know me," Trey said. "Money has never been all that important to me. But that didn't stop your brother from trying to use it to get me away from you."

"So, are you telling me Mason is the reason we broke up? You let him run you?"

His brown eyes darkened as he stared at her.

"Mason vowed to hurt me for touching you from the first minute he found out we were together. Do you think I would let him run me?" He shook his head. "Mason wasn't the one who ran me away, Slim. *You* were."

"Me?"

"You were the only person who could make me leave."

"That is the biggest load of bull—"

"You remember the weekend of your nineteenth birthday?" he asked.

"You mean my nineteenth birthday when I was sick and waited all day for my loving boyfriend to call and wish me a happy birthday?" Kiera bit out through clenched teeth, her body practically vibrating with anger. "I didn't hear from you until the next day, when you called to tell me you'd taken the job at that auto body shop in Houston, a job you told me that you weren't going to take," she said, unable to hide the hurt from her voice.

"You were supposed to come home your birthday weekend," Trey said. The calmness in his tone grated on her nerves. He was acting as though this wasn't one of the most traumatic events of her life.

"I was sick," Kiera reminded him.

"I'd saved an entire paycheck and made reservations for dinner at Emile's, the most expensive place in Gauthier." He continued speaking as if she hadn't said a word. "But then I got that call from you telling me you were sick and that you weren't coming home.

"Your brother had another theory. He came over here to Decker's later that day and insisted that his prediction was coming true. He told me you were pretending to be sick so that you could cancel our plans and hang out with your college friends who were so much better than good-for-nothing me."

"That's not true—" she started, but he cut her off.

"So, I decided to prove him wrong and went to visit you at school that evening."

A sickening feeling filled Kiera's gut as she remembered how hurt she was that Trey hadn't called to wish her a happy birthday. She'd tried to play it off as if it wasn't a big deal, and had even allowed her dorm mates to take her out for pizza.

"I went up to your dorm room with flowers and chicken soup that I made from the recipe you taught me, ready to nurse you back to health," Trey continued. "You can imagine my surprise when I found out from your roommate that you had indeed gone out with friends."

"Trey—"

"So, I went outside and sat on the steps of your dorm. I sat there for three hours, holding a dozen roses and a carton of soup." He looked over at her, his eyes filled with so much hurt Kiera felt it down to her toes. "When you finally came back to your dorm, you and your group of friends walked right past me. You never even noticed me sitting there."

Trembling fingers flew to her lips, but an anguished gasp still escaped.

"Trey—" She started again, but she couldn't

think of what else to say.

"That's when I realized that Mason was right. I was good enough for passing a good time out here at Decker's garage, but I couldn't compete with all that college life had to offer you."

"That's not true," she whispered.

"You were the only thing keeping me in Maplesville, so once I realized I'd lost you, there was no reason to stay. Early the next morning I called that garage in Houston to find out if the job was still available. It was, so I packed up what I could fit in my trunk and was gone within the hour.

"When I got to Houston I thought about turning around and coming right back home, but you know what you said about looking like a fool for chasing after someone who didn't want you?" He shrugged. "So, instead, I called to tell you that it was over. After I ended that call with you, I went to a bar, got sloppy drunk, and met Angie. The rest is history."

He snorted another of those humorless laughs. "It was stupid to think that what had started out as a ploy to piss off your brother could ever turn into something real."

"But it *was* real," Kiera said.

"It never would have worked, Slim, especially once you left for college and saw this whole new world outside of Maplesville."

Kiera wrapped her arms around her middle.

"I didn't know you were there," she said in a small voice.

"It's okay."

"It's not." She shook her head. "I can't imagine how that made you feel."

"It's all good," he said with another shrug.

"Trey, I really was sick that weekend," she said. "I'd only started to feel better later that evening, but it was too late for me to go home to Maplesville. My girlfriends took me out for pizza because I was so upset about you not calling. I'm sorry about what Mason told you. He was wrong."

"Was he? You made it clear from the very beginning that you were using me to get back at Mason, and I was all too happy to be used."

"But it was more than that, Trey. You know it became so much more than that."

"It did." The air between them was heavy with shared regret. "I was in love with you, Kiera. I never expected someone like you would want anything to do with a guy like me. But we clicked. And you…you became my everything."

His softly spoken words sent an arrow of sorrow tearing through her soul.

"I'm just so sorry," she said. "For…for everything. For using you. For blaming you all these years."

"I'm sorry I left without telling you why," he said. "I just thought it was for the best. Mason was right—"

"No, he wasn't," she said.

"Yes, he was, Kiera. You didn't need a guy like me holding you back." He walked up to her and cradled her face in his hands. "The guy I was back then, I wasn't good for you. You deserved better than the old Trey Watson."

She swallowed deeply, her throat clotted with emotion. "What about the new Trey Watson?"

His thumb brushed her cheek. "He's trying to be the kind of man you deserve."

Kiera took his hand from her cheek and kissed his palm. "You're more than enough for me, Trey. You've always been more than enough."

He let out a low groan before dipping his head and capturing her lips in a slow, deep kiss. A mixture of love and passion invaded every corner of her heart, raw and beautiful and powerful. This was Trey as she always wanted him, showing her how he felt with his warm, gentle kiss.

One hand traveled down her waist, settling on her hip, while the other pulled her in closer, encouraging her to bring her body in to his as his tongue glided along the seam of her lips. He sucked on her bottom lip before pushing his tongue into her mouth.

Kiera's soul melted as she lost herself in his kiss. Everything about this moment felt right. It was what she had been missing for so long.

Over the years she had tried to tell herself that she was over him, that Trey Watson was just a boy from her past. She'd convinced herself that the only reason he crept into her mind ever so often was because he was her first love, someone she was destined to remember forever.

But she'd been wrong. He was so much more than that.

Trey was the only man who had ever captured her heart. They had been young, but their love had been real. And in these past few weeks she'd learned how quickly she could fall in love with Trey again.

As she devoured his familiar flavor and experienced that rush he always brought her, Kiera realized that there would never be another man in her life who could measure up to the one in her arms.

He was destined to be her everything.

He became more ardent, his tongue plying her mouth with fiery, passionate kisses. The response from her body was equally passionate as he backed her up against the wall of the garage, her skin tingling with need.

Trey cradled the back of her head with one hand while the other slipped underneath her tank top. His fingers brushed back and forth over her hardening nipple, his thumb and forefinger pinching and plucking until it stood erect. The sensation of the lace bra abrading her skin caused goose bumps to pebble all over

Kiera's body, while another part of her body went liquid.

As if he sensed how much she needed him there in that very moment, Trey wedged his thigh between her legs and rubbed up and down her core. The need to give herself to him completely was overwhelming. She wanted him to have all of her, every single part. Kiera fitted herself more securely against him. She ground her pelvis into his, riding his leg, gasping as he hit all of her sweet spots.

Trey pulled her tank top over her head and tugged her bra cups down, freeing her breasts. He sucked one nipple into his mouth and then the other, deep groans escaping his throat as he went back and forth between the two, giving them equal attention.

His mouth still on her breast, he unsnapped her jeans, and hooked his thumbs over the waistband. As he dragged both her jeans and panties down her legs, his lips followed, peppering her body with wet kisses and long, luxurious licks.

Kiera released a soft moan, her head falling back against the dusty wall as her heart reacted to every spot he touched. With every tender kiss it grew heavier with love for him, until she was sure her heart would burst from her chest.

Trey made his way back up her body and filled her mouth with another deep kiss. With a haste that sent tingles down her spine, he quickly unzipped his own jeans and freed himself from the confines of his boxers, not even bothering to push the jeans down past his hips. He hefted her up, and Kiera wrapped her legs around his waist.

Every inch of her skin tingled, anticipating the moment his thick erection would find its way home. The moment it did, a groan tore from her throat.

"Oh, God," she gasped. She hooked her ankles at the small of his back and crossed her wrists behind his head.

Trey palmed her backside, holding her in place up against the wall as he advanced and retreated, establishing a rhythm that had an orgasm building inside her within seconds. Kiera pitched her head back, staring up at the dilapidated ceiling, but seeing nothing. All she could do was feel.

The fragrance of their lovemaking collided with the faint smell of motor oil still lingering in the air, catapulting her back to that summer when Trey had become her entire world. And here they were, back here, being everything to each other once again.

He buried his face against her neck and sucked, the soft bristles of his barely-there beard stubble abrading her delicate skin. Every nip and bite sent a shot of pleasure coursing through her. With relentless passion he rammed his body into hers, going as far as he could possibly go, until a swift, all-consuming orgasm roared through her bloodstream.

Trey's release soon followed, his limbs trembling as he clutched her to him.

Her head fell forward. She fought for air, her lungs hurting as she tried to inhale. For several moments she couldn't speak, could hardly think.

But there was one thought that would not relent. Despite the mind-numbing pleasure imbuing every part of her brain, it would not let go.

"Trey," she said against his shoulder. "Tell me you forgive me."

He pulled his head back and looked at her. "Forgive you for what?"

"For what happened on my nineteenth birthday. I need to know that you forgive me."

Trey secured his arm underneath her backside and brought his other hand up to cradle the back of her head. He looked into her eyes, his gaze penetrating.

"Slim, I forgave you a long time ago."

Her chest squeezed tight, overwhelmed with emotion. Trey captured her mouth in an achingly tender kiss, his erection once again swelling inside of her.

"There is nothing you can do that I won't forgive, Kiera. That's what happens when you give your heart to someone. You've had mine from the moment you asked me to take you out for hamburgers after the high school football game; I've never truly given it to anyone else."

"I love you so much," she whispered against his lips. "Always, Trey. I have always loved you." She grabbed fistfuls of his shirt as he started to rock inside of her again. He thrust his hips, his thick erection driving deep. Filling her. Stretching her. Touching the very heart of her.

Kiera cried out, the orgasm hitting her with a fierceness that left her breathless.

Hours later, she snuggled up against Trey; wrapped in an old wool blanket he kept in the cab of his truck, she grazed her fingers lightly across the arm he'd draped over her stomach.

"You know what's funny?" she whispered.

"What's that, Slim?"

She looked over her shoulder and smiled at him. "I thought that email from the contest director would be the best thing I got today."

"I guess we still have a lot to celebrate, don't we?" Trey said as he buried his face against her neck. "It's a good thing we've got all night."

Chapter Seven

Kiera stopped short when she spied Trey through the food truck's open back door. Bent over, wiping down the under shelf of the prep table, he provided a view that made her pulse quicken. Her fingers itched to stroke the soft denim hugging his tight butt. She stuck her thumb and index finger between her lips and blew out a loud wolf whistle.

"Lookin' good there." He whipped around, and a cocky grin spread across his face. He was too cocky for his own damn good. "I'm talking about Kiera's Kickin' Kajun," she said.

He climbed out of the truck and pulled her to him. "The hell you are," he said against her lips. "Though I have to say this truck does look damn good."

Kiera nodded, brushing her lips across his. "I love that I can finally show it off. Thanks for driving it over."

Trey had taken the inaugural drive, bringing the food truck from the industrial park to her catering building where it would be parked when not on the road.

"Holy crap, that looks amazing!" Macy's excited voice rang out. They both turned to her. "I can't believe this is the same truck."

Kiera gave her a tour of the interior. Both she and Macy were planning to spend as much time as possible over the next few days testing out the food truck's equipment.

They were down to the wire. The safety inspector was scheduled to arrive in an hour. Once she got through the health inspection, she could head to City Hall to get her operator's permit. It took three days to process the operator's permit, which meant she had to get everything squared away by the end of the day if Kiera's Kickin' Kajun was going to be operational by the start of this weekend's shrimp festival.

As they descended the fold-down steps Trey had installed on the back of the food truck, a late model Chevy Suburban pulled up next to the building.

"That must be the health inspector," Macy said. She held up her crossed fingers. "Good luck," she called as she headed back into the building.

"He's early," Kiera said, shielding her eyes from the sun as she looked toward the SUV.

A cagey smile lined Trey's lips. "That's not the health inspector."

A tall guy wearing a t-shirt with a traffic light on it walked up to them.

"Thanks for coming, Tim," Trey greeted with a handshake. "Kiera, this is Timothy Ryan from the Ready, Set, Geaux Food Truck. He's also part of the New Orleans Food Truck Consortium."

"Yes, of course," Kiera said, shaking the man's outstretched hand. "Your truck is one of the rock stars of the local industry."

"I don't know about that," Tim said. "But we do okay." He nodded toward her truck. "Looks as if you're ready to give me a run for my money. You've got yourself a nice kitchen there."

"Thanks." She tried to curb the huge smile hurting her cheeks, but when the owner of one of New Orleans's hottest food trucks complimented your truck, restraint didn't come easy. "The shrink wrap was finished just yesterday." Kiera took out her cellphone and brought up an old picture of the truck. "You would never believe that it looked like this just a month ago."

Tim's eyes widened as he stared at the phone. He whipped around to Trey. "You did all of this in a month?"

Trey shrugged. "I hired an electrician to do the wiring."

Kiera turned to him and laughed. "Is modesty in the air today or something?" She turned back to Tim and pointed at Trey. "He pulled off the impossible. This truck was a disaster, but he turned it into a thing of beauty, and in record time."

Trey took her hands between his and gave

them a squeeze. "I've been talking to Tim about something he and a few of the other trucks are putting together. Tim, you want to explain?"

He nodded. "A group of us are looking to build a food truck park like the ones in Seattle and Austin. There's a patch of land available for rent in the Bywater area of New Orleans."

Kiera frowned in confusion. "I thought there was an ordinance against a food truck being in one place for longer than two hours?"

"There is, but we're fighting the restaurant association over it. We got the city council to do away with the 600 feet buffer zone around brick and mortar restaurants; we're hopeful they'll do the right thing again. We have nine trucks that have already agreed to join up, but we have space for three more."

"And you want Kiera's Kickin' Kajun?"

"Trey and I have been talking about it this week and we think your Cajun wraps will be a good fit."

"I…I don't know what to say," Kiera said. She looked over at Trey whose eyes were glowing with excitement.

"I've been lurking on some of the food truck message boards and saw some chatter about it. It looked like something you needed to get in on."

Kiera could only manage a small smile. She climbed into the truck and listened as Trey gave Tim a tour of Kiera's Kickin' Kajun's interior.

"This is impressive," Tim said as he looked

around. "And after seeing the before picture, I'm even *more* impressed." He stuck his hand out to Trey. "You do good work. When Ready, Set, Geaux is ready to expand, I know who to call to renovate the next truck."

"Sounds good to me," he said, patting Tim on the back as he walked him to his SUV.

Kiera felt a measure of excitement at the prospect of Trey eventually coming back to work on a food truck for Tim, but she couldn't quell the disquiet settling in her stomach. Discovering that the two of them had apparently spent several days discussing her business without her knowledge didn't sit well with her. She knew Trey meant well with his surprise, but making plans for her food truck without even consulting her?

She had too much business savvy to turn down the offer. Aligning herself with some of the area's most popular food trucks would alleviate a huge part of the burden of getting her name out there, but her gut still churned with unease. This felt reminiscent of too many of those instances when Mason had done what he thought was best for her, without bothering to discuss it with her.

This was *her* business. Trey should have talked to her before ever contacting Timothy Ryan.

Just as she turned to tell him her feelings about it, his cell phone rang.

He looked down at the number, then back up at her. "Can you give me a minute?" He answered the phone. As Kiera listened in on his conversation, the disquiet she was feeling just a minute ago took a back seat as her blood began to pump excitedly through her veins.

Trey looked over at her as he continued to speak into the phone. "I'm going to pay out the remainder of the lease, but I won't be coming back to Houston," he said. "Thanks for everything." He ended the call and slipped the phone into his front pocket. "So much for my surprise."

"You're not going back to Houston?" Kiera asked.

"I was planning to tell you over dinner tonight." He smiled down at her. "I've decided to relocate to Maplesville, permanently. That way I can be close to both you and my kids."

"What about your business?"

"I can run my business from anywhere. There's no reason I have to live in Houston, but there's every reason for me to move back home to Maplesville."

Kiera's chest filled with such joy she was certain it would burst.

"Trey, I love you so much. I love you so much it hurts."

"I know the feeling, baby," he said before gliding his tongue into her mouth. Kiera drank in the sweetness of his kiss, delight rippling through her as Trey masterfully stroked the inside of her mouth.

"Hmm," Kiera said, licking his flavor from her lips. "Do you think we have time to properly celebrate before the health inspector gets here?" she asked, tightening her arms around him and leaning forward, her sights set once again on his delicious mouth.

"Doesn't look like it," Trey said. He gestured with his chin toward another car that had just pulled up. "Maybe we can have a really nice celebration after the truck passes the health inspection."

"I like the way you think," Kiera said.

They broke apart and walked over to greet the health inspector. Trey stood silently by while Kiera conducted the walk-thru. She guided the inspector around the truck, pointing out the safety features, including some steps they'd taken that were beyond what was required to pass the inspection.

"This is a great idea," the inspector said as he studied the three-part compartmentalized cutting board Trey had designed for preventing cross-contamination. "We should require all food prep areas to have one of these."

She looked over at Trey. "Looks as if you may have a new business venture."

"You made this?" the inspector asked him.

Trey nodded, but didn't elaborate.

At first Kiera didn't know what to make of

his modesty, but then she remembered something he'd said in bed last night. He'd told her the rest of this week was her time to shine. He didn't want to take the spotlight off of her.

God, she loved that man.

"Everything looks good, Ms. Coleman," the inspector said. "Give me just a few minutes and I'll issue you your health inspection report."

"Now?"

"Oh yeah." He nodded. "Everything is high-tech these days. I've got the computer and printer in the van. Just give me a minute to input everything and I'll print out your certificate. The results of your inspection will go straight into our computer system."

As soon as she and Trey were alone in the truck, she let out an excited squeal. Holding up her index finger, she said, "One down, one to go. As soon as I have that certificate I can go to the Bureau of Revenue office and get my operating permit."

"It's what you've been working for," Trey said. He planted a kiss on her forehead. "Savor it."

"Ms. Coleman," the inspector called. "Can I see you for a minute?"

Kiera descended the steps and walked over to the back of the inspector's minivan. She tried to ignore the pinprick of panic that struck the back of her neck when she noticed his frown.

"Is everything okay?" she asked.

He pointed to the mounted computer screen. "According to this, you still need to obtain a fire permit. It's separate from the general health and safety inspection."

"Yes, I know. The fire inspection was completed two days ago. Their computers were down so they couldn't issue me the physical permit, but I was assured that it would be filed with the city."

The health inspector shook his head. "It wasn't."

"You've got to be kidding me." Kiera ran both hands through her hair. She let out a ragged sigh. "I guess I can stop by the Fire Prevention Division on my way to City Hall later today."

The frown that deepened the lines on the man's forehead caused the dread already filling her belly to multiply.

"I hate to have to tell you this, but it sounds as if whoever performed the inspection fed you some false information. If it's not on file, it's likely they'll have to perform another fire safety check."

"No way," Kiera said. "I don't have time for that. I have to have everything filed with the state by the end of the day."

"Unless you have some inside connections that can expedite the process, you're out of luck," he said. "Get that fire permit faxed to the Health Department as soon as possible. Our offices are more up-to-date. We can get things done over email and fax. I'm sorry about this," he said before closing the back of the van.

Kiera just stood there as the health inspector slid behind the wheel and backed away. Disappointment and disbelief rendered her motionless.

"I can't believe this," she murmured over and over again. "I just can't believe this."

Trey walked up behind her, captured her shoulders and gave them a firm squeeze. "Don't start thinking the worst, Slim. You can still get this done in time."

"Only if I pull off a miracle. The first thing I need to do is call the Fire Department and tell them about the glitch. Maybe it'll be an easy fix." She blew out another frustrated breath. "What am I talking about? Nothing about this truck has been easy."

"And that's why it's going to be that much more awesome when it's finally on the road," he said.

She pointed to his watch. "I have three hours before the Bureau of Revenue closes. How am I going to get all of this done in time?"

"You heard what the inspector said." Trey hesitated a moment, then, shaking his head, said, "You need help from someone with connections. I can't believe I'm about to say this, but I think you need to call a certain someone and have him call in a favor."

"No." Kiera shook her head. "I'm not calling Mason."

"Slim, if there was ever a time *not* to be stubborn, this would be the time. I'm the last person who would encourage you to ask him for anything, but Mason is a well-connected attorney. Hell, just the other day he said he was meeting with Senator Gauthier. Have him call in a favor."

"No," she reiterated.

Mason's favorite pastime was bailing her out of messes, but she refused to run to him like some helpless baby sister who needed her big brother to fix things once again. Especially after the way he'd thrown that loan in her face. But the loan was only a part of it. After learning the part her brother had played in her break up with Trey all those years ago, putting it in Trey's mind that Kiera was in some way ashamed of him, she wasn't sure she could handle seeing Mason without knocking him upside the head.

This was *her* problem. She would take care of it.

She dislodged herself from Trey's hold. "I need to go."

"Call your brother."

She looked up at him and shook her head again. "I'll figure something out."

"Kiera—" He reached for her, but she sidestepped him.

"Please, Trey." She held her hands up. "Let

me handle this. It's my problem, I'll figure out a way to solve it."

With that Kiera took off for her car, hoping against hope that she really could pull off a miracle.

Trey spotted Mason standing next to a gleaming black Mercedes-Benz parked in one of the slanted spots across from City Hall in downtown New Orleans. He pulled in next to it and had to fight the urge not to open his door a little too wide and scrap the side of the car.

You're better than that, Trey reminded himself. He wouldn't allow his last run-in with Mason to turn him back into the reckless hothead he used to be. He'd been trying too hard over this past month to convince Kiera that he was a different man—a *better* man.

And right now he needed Mason Coleman.

Actually, his sister needed him, but for some reason she'd decided to toss her hat in the ring for the title of World's Most Stubborn Woman. Trey couldn't allow her stubbornness to get in the way of everything she'd worked so hard for leading up to this weekend's festival, so he'd swallowed every bitter drop of his pride and called Mason himself.

Trey got out of his truck and walked over to Mason, who was talking on his cellphone.

"Do you have everything?" Trey asked him.

Mason held up a finger—one that happened *not* to be his middle finger. Maybe they were making progress.

"Yeah, I'll be back in the office in a half hour, hopefully sooner," he said to the person on the other end of the line. He ended the call and lifted his briefcase. "The Health Department faxed over the inspection certificate ten minutes ago. I got here as quickly as I could."

"Good," Trey said. He glanced at his watch as they climbed the set of stone steps leading to the entrance. "We have less than ten minutes to get the paperwork filed. You sure your buddy is going to be able to do it even without Kiera's signature?"

"I told him she'll be here to sign it first thing in the morning. He's going to have his personal assistant input everything into the computer system so they can get the process started. Kiera should still get the permit by Friday."

"Thank God," Trey breathed, opening the door so Mason could enter ahead of him.

He walked into the building and stopped dead in his tracks.

Amid the throng of people hustling around the spacious lobby, there stood Kiera, her gaze traveling back and forth between him and Mason.

"What are you two doing here?" Her eyes narrowed, her brow furrowing as realization dawned. "You called Mason?"

"I thought you needed him, Kiera," Trey said.

"The question is why didn't *you* call me?" Mason asked. "You knew I could take care of this with a couple of phone calls."

"Because I didn't want you involved! Dammit, Trey!" she said loud enough to draw stares.

Trey reached for her, but she yanked her arm away and stormed out of the door they'd just entered. He took off after her, catching her before she could reach the steps.

"Would you let me explain?" he asked, tugging her out of the flow of foot traffic. He was relieved when she let him lead her over to one of the stone flowerpots ornamenting the dais that surrounded the building. "I called Mason—"

"After I specifically told you I didn't want to," she said. "Aren't *you* the one who keeps telling me I should stop relying on Mason because all he wants to do is control me?"

"You said that about me?" Mason asked as he joined them. "Now do you see why I don't like you? Asshole."

"Shut up, Mason," Kiera shot at her brother.

Trey held both hands up. "Look, Slim, you can yell at me all you want, but can't it wait until after you get everything straight for your operator's permit?"

She held up a sheaf of papers. "Why do you think I'm here?"

Trey stared at the documents. "How'd you get that done?"

"Because the glitch was in the health inspector's computer system, not the fire department's. My fire permit was on file just like they told me it would be."

"Shit, Kiera, why didn't you tell me?"

"Because I told you I was handling it."

"So, is everything okay here?" Mason asked as he typed away on his phone. "Because I've got a meeting I need to get back to."

"No one asked you to come."

"He asked me." He nudged his head toward Trey. "I still don't like your ass, but thanks for looking out for her."

"Whatever," Trey said.

"Asshole," they both said under their breath.

Mason kissed Kiera's cheek and then started for his car. Kiera's expression remained hostile as she watched her brother walk away. Trey didn't say anything. He figured the longer she had to cool off, the better for him.

His reprieve didn't last long.

She turned her attention back to him. "I can't believe you," she said.

Trey held his hands up again. "I was only trying to help, Kiera. I didn't want anything coming between you and the success you've been banking on at this weekend's festival. I knew with all his connections Mason would be able to grease the skids if necessary."

She crossed her arms over her chest. "Do you know how many times Mason offered to fly someone in to work on the truck, or to hire someone to drive it to any of a number of custom renovation companies throughout the country? He even ordered a fully outfitted truck; paid nearly $90,000 for it. If it weren't for Jada tipping me off to what he'd done in time for me to cancel the order, it would have been delivered months ago.

"This food truck does mean a lot to me, Trey. And, yes, I'm hoping this coming weekend will be a huge success, but it won't mean anything if *I'm* not the reason it's a success. I've spent my entire life counting on other people to do things for me. I wanted to do this on my own. For you, of all people, to be the one to drag Mason into this."

The disappointment and hurt he saw in her dark brown eyes was like a punch to the gut.

"Kiera, I never wanted to take anything away from you. I swear I was only trying to help."

"Is that what you called yourself doing when you lied to me about just how much the materials for the flooring cost?" Trey's head reared back. "I found the receipt in your truck the other night," she said. "And I supposed you were only helping me when you started making plans for my truck with Timothy Ryan?"

"I knew money was an issue and I didn't want you stopping the renovation because you couldn't afford the new flooring," he said. "And I contacted Tim because joining that consortium is a golden opportunity. If you don't want to join it, why did you tell Tim you would?"

"I didn't say I didn't want to join it. I would be a fool not to, but dammit, Trey, don't you think you should have at least asked me? You accuse me of allowing Mason to make my decisions for me, and then you go ahead and do the exact same thing."

Her words slapped him in the face.

Son of a bitch.

She was right. He'd criticized her brother for trying to control her life, yet here he was teaming up with Mason so they could both take care of her.

"Dammit," Trey said in a harsh whisper. How had he not seen this?

Kiera slapped her hand to her chest. "This is *mine*, Trey. It's my turn. I need to be the reason for my own success."

The quaver in her voice completely gutted him.

"You are. Make no mistake about it; *you* made this happen, Kiera. Not me. Not Mason. *You.*" He took a chance and reached for her hand. "I'm sorry. I shouldn't have contacted Mason behind your back. I shouldn't have contacted Tim Ryan without talking to you about it first."

The fear that he'd messed things up with her caused Trey's chest to tighten with panic. Using the words she'd said to him as they'd made love at Decker's garage, Trey whispered, "Tell me that you forgive me. Even if you can't do it yet, I need to know that you'll eventually forgive me."

She looked up at him. After some of the tensest seconds of his life passed, she finally said, "I guess it's only fair. You did, after all, give me the last of your root beer float."

The relief that crashed through him made his knees go weak. Trey pulled her against him, crushing her to his chest.

"Thank you," he whispered against the top of her head. "Thank you, Kiera."

"Just promise me that you won't do anything like this again."

"I swear it," he said.

"Good," she whispered against his chest. "Trey?"

"Hmm?" he murmured.

"I need you to make me another promise."

"Anything."

She looked up at him. "Don't leave me again. Ever."

"That's the easiest promise you could ever ask me to make. I'm not going anywhere, Slim. I'm here for you, always.

Epilogue

Displaying her ribbon, Kiera took a couple of steps to the right, huddling in with the first and second place winners of the shrimp cook-off. Once the photographer indicated he had what he needed, she hurried from the stage and down the steps to the entourage waiting for her. Jada and Callie gathered her in a group hug.

"Congratulations, honey!" Callie said, kissing her cheek. "I still think you should have won first place, but competition was stiff."

"Maybe second place," Kiera said. "Even I have to admit that the Szechuan-Honey Shrimp deserved the top prize."

"As far as I can tell, coming in third isn't hurting business over at Kiera's Kickin' Kajun," Jada pointed out. "That line has been at least twenty-people long for the last two hours."

"I know!" Kiera said. "I've been keeping an eye on it. Macy and the crew must be exhausted, but I am *loving* it!"

Mason walked over to them with an ice cream cone in one hand and a stuffed teddy bear in the other. "Look what I won you, baby. Cute, huh?" he said, handing the stuffed animal to Jada.

She took the peace offering, but not before sending him a menacing frown.

Mason blew out an agitated breath. "Even Kiera has forgiven me, Jada."

"She's nicer than I am," his fiancée answered.

He rolled his eyes, then wrapped Kiera up in a hug. "Congratulations. I'm proud of you."

"I would have liked to have won the big prize," she said, returning his hug. "But third place isn't so bad."

"Third place is awesome, and you know I'm not only talking about this contest when I say I'm proud of you." He kissed the top of her head. "I'm proud of everything you've accomplished here. And in case I haven't said it enough, I'm sorry."

Emotion lodged in her throat. As often as she wanted to do him bodily harm for his meddling, making her big brother proud would always mean the world to her.

Mason had come over to her kitchen last night to see how things were going. Kiera had stopped in the middle of preparations for the day's contest to discuss Mason's role in her break up with Trey fourteen years ago.

Her brother had been contrite, something Kiera rarely saw from him. Forgiving him had been easier than she thought it would be, undoubtedly because now she knew Trey was hers. Forever this time.

"Thank you," she said, giving him another hug. "And you *are* taking the $3,000 I won for coming in third place."

Her brother remained silent.

"Mason…" Kiera said in a warning tone.

"Whatever," he growled.

Mychal responded to her text about her win a few minutes later. When she discovered he was on the way to the hospital with Naomi, who was in labor, Kiera chewed him out, then threatened to punch him in the stomach if she didn't get a picture of the new baby as soon as it made its world debut.

She ended the call with Mychal, turned and found Trey standing a few feet away with Rachel and Roland Jr. at his side. Just like that, her entire world brightened.

"Hey there," Kiera said in greeting.

Trey gestured to the kids. "They wanted to congratulate you before going on the carnival rides."

Both kids gave her hugs, and Kiera felt her throat tighten again.

They took off for the Tilt-A-Whirl, leaving she and Trey behind. His smile ramped up to mega-wattage strength as he sauntered up to her and wrapped his arms around her waist. He gave her a chaste kiss on the tip of her nose.

"Congratulations, Slim. You did a good job."

She grimaced. "Third place. Not quite what I was hoping for, but better than all those honorable mentions."

"Hey, third place is nothing to sneeze at. You beat out some stiff competition." He linked his hands at the small of her back. "You should be proud of yourself."

"I am. I just wish I'd beat out a couple more. I really wanted that top prize."

"You don't have anything to worry about. I predict Kiera's Kickin' Kajun is going to bring in twice what that prize was worth in the first few months. Now that people have gotten a little taste of what you have to offer, they'll be hooked."

"You really think that's all it'll take?"

"Oh, yeah, Slim." He leaned over and planted a kiss on her lips. "That's all it took to get me hooked. Just a little taste."

Thank you so much for purchasing and reading ***Just A Little Taste***.

If you haven't done so yet, be sure to read Callie and Stefan's love story in the first novella of the *Moments in Maplesville* series, ***A Perfect Holiday Fling*** and Jada and Mason's story in ***A Little Bit Naughty.***

The Holmes Brother Series:

Set in New Orleans, the Holmes Brothers series follows the lives of Elijah, Tobias, and Alexander Holmes as they find love in one of the world's most romantic cities.

Read ***Deliver Me, Release Me***, and ***Rescue Me***, available both individually and in a special bundle edition!
Get all three books in the Holmes Brothers series for one low price!

In Her Wildest Dreams

Event planner Erica Cole recruits her best friend to help her plan the ultimate Valentine's Day fantasy, but chocolatier Gavin Foster is determined to show her that they should be more than just friends.

The Rebound Guy

Relationship advisor Dexter Bryant is trying to shake his stud-for-hire image, but when Asia Carpenter makes him an offer he can't refuse, Dex will have to play the role of professional rebound guy one last time.

Romances from Harlequin Kimani!

The New York Sabers

Don't miss my sizzling ***New York Sabers*** *football series! Check my website for details!*

Bayou Dreams

Check out my brand new series set in the small, fictional town of Gauthier, Louisiana!

About the Author:

A native of south Louisiana, *USA Today* Bestselling author Farrah Rochon officially began her writing career while waiting in between classes in the student lounge at Xavier University of Louisiana. After earning her Bachelors of Science degree and a Masters of Arts from Southeastern Louisiana University, Farrah decided to pursue her lifelong dream of becoming a published novelist. She was named *Shades of Romance Magazine*'s Best New Author of 2007. Her debut novel garnered rave reviews, earning Farrah several SORMAG Readers' Choice Awards. *I'll Catch You*, the second book in her New York Sabers series for Harlequin Kimani, was a 2012 RITA(R) Award finalist.

When she is not writing in her favorite coffee shop, Farrah spends most of her time reading her favorite romance novels or seeing as many Broadway shows as possible. An admitted sports fanatic, Farrah feeds her addiction to football by watching New Orleans Saints games on Sunday afternoons.